"Who's there?" Drew called out.

Sweat broke out when he heard the cock of a shotgun.

With a fast reflex, Drew hooked the ankle of the intruder and they landed hard on the dirt floor. He heard the rush of air from the woman's lungs.

And her sputtering.

He felt like laughing.

Olivia.

What the hell was she doing here?

"Drew!" Her voice registered amazement; then she laughed, relaxing under his weight. "Oh, I'm so sorry—I didn't mean to hurt you."

"You didn't hurt me," he said. "In case you haven't noticed, I won that round."

"I don't think so."

Unable to resist, Drew dipped his head and kissed her, stealing her breath before she could catch it and talk back.

When her arms crept around his neck, he knew he'd won this minor skirmish, but not the entire battle!

Dear Reader,

Instead of writing your resolutions, I have the perfect way to begin the new year—read this month's spectacular selection of Silhouette Special Edition romances! These exciting books will put a song in your heart, starting with another installment of our very popular MONTANA MAVERICKS series—*In Love With Her Boss* by the stellar Christie Ridgway. Christie vows this year to "appreciate the time I have with my husband and sons and appreciate *them* for the unique people they are."

Lindsay McKenna brings us a thrilling story from her MORGAN'S MERCENARIES: DESTINY'S WOMEN series with *Woman of Innocence*, in which an adventure-seeking beauty meets up with the legendary—and breathtaking—mercenary of her dreams! The excitement continues with Victoria Pade's next tale, *On Pins and Needles*, in her A RANCHING FAMILY series. Here, a skeptical sheriff falls for a lovely acupuncturist who finds the wonder cure for all his doubts—her love!

And what does a small-town schoolteacher do when she finds a baby on her doorstep? Find out in Nikki Benjamin's heartwarming reunion romance *Rookie Cop*. A love story you're sure to savor is *The Older Woman* by Cheryl Reavis, in which a paratrooper captain falls head over heels for the tough-talking nurse living next door. This year, Cheryl wants to "stop and smell the roses." I also recommend Lisette Belisle's latest marriage-of-convenience story, *The Wedding Bargain*, in which an inheritance—and two hearts—are at stake! Lisette believes that the new year means "a fresh start, and vows to meet each new day with renewed faith, energy and a sense of humor."

I'm pleased to celebrate with you the beginning of a brand-new year. May you also stop to smell the roses, and find many treasures in Silhouette Special Edition the whole year through!

Enjoy!

Karen Taylor Richman
Senior Editor

The Wedding Bargain

LISETTE BELISLE

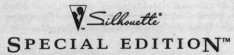

SPECIAL EDITION™

Published by Silhouette Books

America's Publisher of Contemporary Romance

With heartfelt thanks to my agent, Karen Solem,
for reasons too numerous to list.

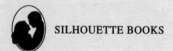 SILHOUETTE BOOKS

ISBN 0-373-24446-0

THE WEDDING BARGAIN

Copyright © 2002 by Lisette Belisle

Visit Silhouette at www.eHarlequin.com

Printed in U.S.A.

Books by Lisette Belisle

Silhouette Special Edition

Just Jessie #1134
Her Sister's Secret Son #1403
The Wedding Bargain #1446

LISETTE BELISLE

believes in putting everything into whatever she does,
whether it's a nursing career, motherhood or writing.
While balancing a sense of practicality with a streak of
adventure, she applies that dedication in creating stories
of people overcoming the odds. Her message is clear—
believe in yourself and believe in love. She is the founder
and past president of the Saratoga chapter of Romance
Writers of America. Canadian-born, she grew up in New
Hampshire and currently lives in upstate New York with
her engineer husband, Frank.

She'd love to hear from her readers. She can be reached
at: P.O. Box 1166, Ballston Lake, NY 12019.

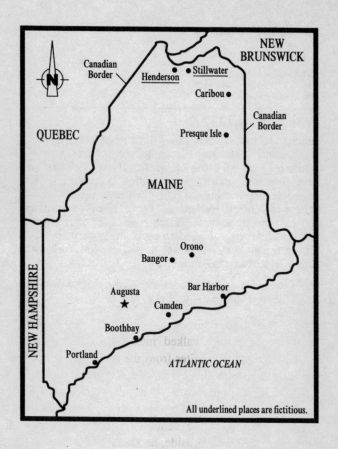

NEW BRUNSWICK

Canadian Border

<u>Henderson</u> • <u>Stillwater</u>

Caribou •

Canadian Border

QUEBEC

Presque Isle •

MAINE

NEW HAMPSHIRE

Orono

Bangor •

Bar Harbor •

Augusta ★ Camden •

Boothbay •

Portland • ATLANTIC OCEAN

All underlined places are fictitious.

Chapter One

It felt strange to be free.

Free.

Five years after an explosion ripped his world apart, Drew Pierce walked into a roadside diner. Seeking temporary shelter from the rain, and the descending night, he blended in with the rough crowd.

His clothes felt damp, they were cheap, free prison issue, no name brands. His mouth twisted, recalling a time when that had actually mattered to him. Shrugging the thought aside, he skirted the occupied tables and found a seat at the chrome-edged counter. He sat on a hard stool, aware of a certain weariness that had nothing to do with time and circumstances.

His last ride had dropped him off at the diner. After a short break he'd be on the road again, hitching a ride with one of the truck drivers going his way. He was going home, surely a time for rejoicing. But no one was cheering, least of all him.

A middle-aged waitress was flipping burgers; onions sizzled on the grill. She looked dead on her feet; nevertheless, she spared him a smile. "What'll it be?"

Drew stared back blankly. It had been so long since anyone had offered him a choice.

Choices.

He'd made so many wrong ones. They'd brought him to this place…this moment in time. The fluorescent lights were dim with several bulbs burned out. The day's menu—meat loaf, mashed potatoes and green beans, along with the usual fare of burgers and deli-type selections—was posted on a chalkboard. The diner was definitely not a four-star establishment. He'd hit rock bottom.

The waitress was waiting for his order.

"Just coffee—black." He raised his voice above the music blaring out of the jukebox. He didn't recognize the tune, but it was pure country.

"You want anything to go with that?"

"That's it," Drew replied, with his thin wallet in mind. He barely had enough money to last a couple more days. His empty stomach groaned in protest. His gaze drifted hungrily to the pie sitting under glass. The crust was thin, the filling thick, purple-blue.

The waitress followed his glance. "We're closing soon. The last piece is half-price." Her kindness surprised Drew.

Swallowing his pride, he murmured, "Thanks."

Moments later he bit into the generous wedge of pie. Yes, the blueberries were just as wild and sweet as he remembered, like forbidden fruit, some of northern Maine's finest, no doubt. The coffee was strong, just the way he liked it—not that he would have complained.

He'd learned to accept small inconveniences, small indignities, even the big ones, to be honest. And he was nothing if not honest—a hard-won lesson. With everything stripped away, he'd taken a hard look at himself and didn't like what he'd seen— a careless playboy, a user. His father had always said his second son would come to a bad end; and Drew had proved him right.

He polished off the last bite of pie.

In the corner, a television set was tuned to a football game. A few men had gathered around. Drew glanced at it idly. Someone turned up the volume a notch or two, competing with the jukebox and the sounds of laughter and conversation.

When the noise abruptly leveled off, Drew was slow to react. Lifting his cup to his mouth, he didn't turn to gape at the new arrival as the other men did; nevertheless, he couldn't tear his gaze away from the woman's reflection in the mirror behind the counter. Through a smoke-filled haze, he got an eyeful.

He'd heard the saying "Good things come in small packages." Small and slender in a black leather jacket, with tight black jeans tucked into leather boots, she was dynamite.

For a brief charged minute, their gazes connected in the mirror. Something warm kindled in her eyes before she glanced away. With a stifled inner groan, Drew tried to deny his gut reaction. How long had it been since he'd been within touching distance of a beautiful sexy woman?

Too long.

When she drew off a cap to reveal a glorious tangle of pale golden hair, a man sitting near Drew was lighting a cigarette. The match flared, then burned down while she shook the moisture from her head, then walked slowly forward—every move as graceful as a small sinewy cat.

"Ouch!" The match burned the man's fingers.

With a wry smile, Drew knew exactly how the man felt. She was hot. Once, he would have tried to pick her up. Now, he buried the impulse and nursed his coffee. He'd sown his wild oats, and then some. From now on, he intended to be the soul of discretion and stay out of trouble.

And she looked like his definition of trouble!

Apart from that, she looked youthful, a little unsure. Drew hoped she knew how to handle herself with this crowd because he had no intention of coming to her rescue. The tension in the room was palpable. And all because of a little piece of fluff.

She looked fragile, yet ripe.

With a frown, Drew silenced the thought.

The lights dimmed slightly.

The waitress called, "Closing in ten."

Olivia DeAngelis heard the announcement.

Just her luck, she thought. With a sinking feeling, she took in the scene. The diner was closing. And here she was, stranded, somewhere south of Presque Isle.

She had planned to stay overnight in Bangor. But disheartened after seeing her lawyer and receiving his less-than-encouraging summary of her finances—and what she could do about it—she'd changed her mind and decided to head home despite the bad driving weather.

Now, to make matters worse, she'd stumbled into a diner filled with hard-core bikers and truckers. There wasn't a respectable-looking man in sight, she decided, automatically rating each man according to his general appearance.

When she found her gaze tangling a second time with a pair of brooding dark eyes reflected in the mirror behind the counter, she wondered—had she sunk low enough to consider a stranger met in a seedy diner? She flushed at the thought and watched his eyes narrow. Had he read her mind?

Hastily she looked away.

At the moment, she had more pressing concerns than finding a husband to satisfy her lawyer. How to get home topped her list.

While she hesitated, one man broke from a group around the television. "Hey, doll, need some company?"

Trying to appear casual, she smiled. "No, thanks, I'm meeting someone." She wasn't, but he didn't have to know that.

"Don't rush off."

Olivia felt a big beefy hand on her arm. "Excuse me," she said, dismissing him more firmly.

The man chuckled through his thick pepper-gray beard, but he didn't loosen his hold. "Forget your date. How about a drink?"

Olivia looked around for an escape. Her gaze fell again on the lone man at the far end of the counter. While all the other men were watching with avid attention, he was ignoring her—which made him appear safe.

"There's my date." She disguised her clamoring nerves with a light laugh. Forcing herself not to run, she crossed the room.

"Hey," the man called after her. "Not so fast."

Olivia didn't slow down. Taking a deep breath, she slid onto the empty stool beside the stranger, then leaned toward him.

"Please, pretend you know me," she whispered, momentarily shaken by the shuttered cynicism in his dark-brown eyes when he turned to look at her. "Just for a couple of minutes."

Meeting her plea with an unwelcoming frown, he released a harsh sigh with the words, "I don't want any trouble."

"Neither do I." She met his dark gaze.

He shook his head. "Look, I'm no knight in shining armor. Why don't you find someone else?"

She looked around. "Who do you recommend?"

"Hell," he muttered, then fell silent.

Taking that as an agreement, Olivia relaxed...a little.

The waitress glanced at both of them. "Who's buying?"

"I am," Olivia spoke up brightly. Thanks to a difficult childhood, she'd learned to take care of herself. Adapting to any new situation was lesson number one.

With a trail of unhappy children and broken marriages left behind, Olivia's mother had spent her life trying to find herself—usually through some man.

Sadly she never had.

For the most part, Olivia avoided the male half of the species. It wasn't that she didn't like men; she simply didn't want one of her own.

However, she'd learned to rely on her intuition

when all else failed her. Some basic instinct told her that her rescuer—no matter how reluctant, aloof and unsociable—would do her no harm.

Under the dim lights, his face appeared shadowed; his hair was dark, clipped short. His clothes looked as if they belonged to someone else—someone stockier. He looked down on his luck. Olivia could identify with that. In less than six months, she'd be homeless.

Putting the dismal reality aside, she glanced at his drink, surprised to see it was nonalcoholic.

"I'll have a Coke," she said to the waitress, while ignoring the stranger's lack of enthusiasm about her company. "I'm starved. Can I have some chips with that? I've been on the road all day. The weather's awful! Then, to top it off, my car's been acting funny since I left Bangor." Olivia stopped just long enough to take a much-needed breath. "I don't suppose there's anyone here who can fix it?"

"Not until morning, I'm afraid." The waitress took a swipe at the counter with a damp sponge. "A mechanic usually comes on duty at the garage next door at eight. There's a motel out back. It's nothing special," she added.

Olivia could just imagine a seedy motel. They probably charged by the hour. "I was hoping to get home tonight."

She jumped when the stranger at her side spoke up.

"Where's home?" he asked.

"Henderson. It's not far, less than two hours away."

He raised an eyebrow. "I know where it is."

"Oh?" When he said nothing more, she spoke

again, "By the way, my name's Olivia DeAngelis. And you are?"

"Drew Pierce." He seemed to wait for a reaction—obviously assuming she recognized the name.

Returning with Olivia's order, the waitress provided a distraction. She looked at Drew with interest.

"My husband used to do some logging. You related to them Pierces?"

"Yes," he responded.

Amused by the terse reply, Olivia raised her glass to her lips, hiding her surprise at his identity. So this was the infamous Drew Pierce. Of course, she'd heard of him.

The Pierce family had once controlled Henderson's logging and farming economy, before an explosion destroyed the migrant camp. Olivia frowned, trying to recall the details of the trial that followed—something about safety violations. There were also charges of mismanagement. Despite some high-powered lawyers, Drew Pierce was found guilty and sentenced, after which his family had cut their losses and left Henderson. The town hadn't been the same since.

Olivia glanced at him, taking in the square chin, the full sensuous mouth, the dark hair and eyes. Funny, he didn't look like pond scum, or any other of the unflattering terms she'd heard used around town to describe him. In fact, he looked disturbingly handsome in a reckless, edgy sort of way.

Then she remembered something else.

His family might have left town, but their house, Oakridge, was still standing. They were practically neighbors! She almost said as much, but his closed expression suggested he wouldn't welcome that piece of information.

Olivia opened the bag of chips and offered him some.

"No thanks." Drew tried to ignore her.

He really did try.

Might as well try to ignore a fly buzzing around his ear, he decided. But with her laughter and lightness, she seemed so feminine, so new, reminding him of all the female company he'd missed. If he stayed here one moment longer, he'd be demanding a key to that motel room and trying to lure her out there. But he didn't do that sort of thing anymore! He was reformed, determined to go straight and avoid any entanglements, even if it killed him. Which meant he needed to rescue her—if only from himself.

With that thought uppermost, he said, "I know something about cars. Let me take a look."

"Thanks." She sounded breathless, as if he'd surprised her.

He probably had—he'd shocked himself. He wasn't sure why he felt the need to help her. Maybe it was that vulnerable mouth or the determined cheerfulness…or the way she filled out her jeans. In any case, the sooner he fixed her car and sent her on her way, the better he would feel.

He held out his hand. "Can I have the keys?"

She started to hand them to him, then stopped. "I think I'll come with you."

So she wasn't all that trusting.

Smart woman.

With a tight smile, Drew took the keys from her, got up, then walked out, not surprised when she hastened after him. He didn't slow down until he reached the parking lot.

The truck stop was all lit up with glittering red and blue neon lights. Rain bounced off the pavement. Within seconds, he was drenched.

Great.

With a grimace of discomfort, Drew turned up the collar of his denim jacket. It wasn't waterproof.

Through the downpour, he looked around the parking lot. "Which car is yours?"

She pointed to a sedan sandwiched between two eighteen-wheel trucks. "That one." Her car was small, like her, and a pale powder-blue.

With Olivia looking on, Drew climbed into the driver's seat, then turned the ignition. Nothing happened.

"When did you first notice something was wrong?" he asked.

In response, she spared him none of the details. "It was running fine when I left Bangor after dropping off my brother and his family at the airport. Then I had lunch and did a couple of errands. It all took longer than I hoped. The car was still fine when I started driving home. Then it got dark."

"Then what?"

"When I turned on the lights, they were dim. And they got dimmer. I'm lucky I got this far."

Lucky for whom?

Sorting through all the information, Drew said, "Sounds like the battery might be going. How old is it?"

She looked at the car. "I bought it secondhand."

"When was that?"

"About four years ago. They said all the equipment was original.'' She beamed—as if that was a good thing.

Drew grunted some response. Her optimism was beginning to wear thin. ''Let's have a look.'' He propped the hood open, then bent over the engine. ''The battery terminals look corroded.''

''Hmm.'' She got out an umbrella—a yellow flowered one, then tried to hold it steady over his head while he cleaned the terminals. The wind blew, rain lashed in four directions.

Before long, they were both soaked. She sneezed.

Drew glanced at her. ''Why don't you go back inside?''

''You might need my help.'' She smiled at him, her eyes wide and gray, as crystal clear and guileless as a mountain stream.

He stared for a long moment. Something about her seemed familiar. ''What did you say your name was?''

''Olivia DeAngelis.''

His gaze skimmed over her delicate flower-face, her pale hair. Irrepressible as her, it curled like a gold halo around her head. ''You don't look Italian.''

In her black leather jacket and jeans, she was an intriguing blend of worldliness and innocence. A wayward angel.

''I'm not. I was adopted.'' She didn't add any details.

''You're not from around here originally.''

She tilted her head. ''How did you guess?''

''The accent gave you away.'' He'd gone to college and met people from the West Coast. ''California breeze.''

She laughed. ''I'm not sure that's a compliment.''

When he remained silent, her smile faded.

So he'd finally burst her bubble of cheer. In a way, Drew regretted it, but perhaps it was just as well. He didn't need a woman like her cluttering his life. He had no connections; his family had disowned him. Under the circumstances, he didn't really blame them. His list of transgressions was long.

He'd hurt some innocent people and served time in an out-of-state minimum-security prison—not his idea of a country club by any stretch of the imagination. Society had exacted a price, and he'd paid. Would that satisfy his detractors and earn forgiveness? He was going home to face the same people who judged him guilty and sent him to prison. Beyond that, he had no plans—except to pick up his few belongings, then head out somewhere.

He had no clear destination in mind—as long as it was as far from his past as he could get.

Only one thing was certain—no one would miss him.

Not a soul.

Did he care?

He wasn't sure. The admission left him empty.

At his deliberate attempt to distance himself, Olivia shivered in the cold autumn night. She tried to shake off Drew's easy dismissal. People usually liked her; she worked hard to make sure they did.

Unexpectedly hurt and not willing to examine the reason too closely since all six-foot-two of him was standing less than a yard away, she decided to treat his rudeness with silence. That lasted about a minute.

Now he was glowering at the engine!

Alarmed, she leaned over for a closer look—brushing his hard elbow with her own.

"What's wrong with it?" she asked, confused by the mess of greasy gears and wires.

"Nothing." He inched his arm away, leaving her feeling colder than before. "I just cleaned and reset the wires. With a jump-start, you can be on your way."

"Oh." What had she expected?

Surprisingly he gave her a direct glance. "Look, I'm sorry if I've been rude."

His mouth was set in a rigid line, his brow was furrowed. He didn't look sorry. His chiseled features looked hard, with deep-set eyes that looked older than the rest of him. Despite that bit of insight, Olivia hardened her sympathetic heart.

She didn't flinch from the truth. "You think I'm an airhead." Why did that hurt? Why should she care what this man thought? She'd survived worse.

Drew heard the defensive note in her voice. "I didn't say that." All right, so maybe he did think she was a mental lightweight. He couldn't deny that. But he also thought she was very young—far too young and vulnerable to be out alone, forced to rely on strangers for help.

If she belonged to him, he'd—

He stopped the thought before it went anywhere.

She wasn't his. There had been many women in his life, but only one had touched his heart and left it permanently scarred. There was no room for another, which was exactly the way he wanted it.

Wasn't it?

Before they got mired any deeper in this conversation, Drew decided to put an end to it. "Look, I didn't mean to offend you."

She lifted her dainty chin. "You didn't."

He tried to keep a note of impatience from creeping into his voice. "I don't know you. I offered to fix your car. That's it. We're never going to see each other again, so my opinion hardly matters. Does it?"

Her heart-shaped face, with delicate brows and mouth, remained soft—even though she was visibly annoyed. "No, it doesn't."

At her aggrieved tone, he hid a smile.

"Then how about handing me that wrench?" He held out his hand.

"This one?" She slapped the hard metal into his outstretched palm.

The impact stung.

"Thanks," he said dryly. Despite her diminutive size, Olivia DeAngelis packed a wallop.

"I think I'll wait in the car." She coolly folded her umbrella, then turned away.

In silence Drew watched her climb into the car, firmly resisting the urge to call her back, to apologize. He winced when she slammed the door.

Drew bent to his task again. Moments later, a trucker stopped and offered the use of his jumper cables. Before long, with the battery recharged, the car started on the first try. Drew dropped the hood with a satisfied "thud." With a tip of his hat, the trucker drove away.

"Guess that does it." Drew wiped his hands on a rag.

Olivia sat in the driver's seat. Unsmiling, she rolled down the window. "Thank you so much for your help. I'd like to pay you something for your trouble."

At her offer, Drew backed away. "No thanks."

Olivia frowned, her fine brows arched. "But I would have paid a mechanic."

Drew shook his head, absorbing the fact that she was different from so many women he'd known in his life who wanted something from him. Being broke eliminated that worry.

"It's not necessary." He wouldn't accept money from her, even though he could use it. The fact that she'd probably guessed stung his pride.

But when he looked into her wide gray eyes, he didn't see pity, just understanding. Acceptance. He was down on his luck, there was no hiding it.

After a lifetime of trying to live up to everyone's expectations, and failing badly, Drew was free of the Pierce wealth, free of all the family trappings—which left him in the middle of nowhere—with the lonely night bearing down on him with each passing second, and the rain carrying the cold sting of autumn.

"Thank you," she said simply.

"You're welcome." With an ironic smile, Drew turned away, leaving her with a half-mocking, "So long, Angel."

Chapter Two

Angel.

Olivia smiled ruefully.

He'd obviously forgotten her name.

She didn't watch him walk away. She refused to let his careless dismissal hurt. No matter how intriguing, Drew Pierce was nothing more than a passing stranger—and not a very friendly one at that.

Men like him were good at one thing—walking away from a woman. She wasn't sure how she knew that after such a brief encounter, but she did. Her smooth brow knit into a pensive frown. It occurred to her that Drew was the type of man who would make an ideal husband for her purposes—an absent one.

Despite the obvious benefits of such an arrangement, Olivia shuddered at the mere thought of marriage as a clear-cut business arrangement, even a temporary one. It was unthinkable, but then, so was losing Stone's End.

When the wind blew a few fat drops of rain through the open car window, she rolled it up, then turned on the heat, along with the radio. Warm air took off the chill, soft music poured into the silent void, drowning out her troubled thoughts.

She didn't want to think beyond getting to Stone's End—while she could still call it home. Unless she could find a legal method to break her birth father's will, it wouldn't be home much longer. Had she found Stone's End only to lose it?

At the age of nineteen, she'd connected with her birth family through a detective the family had hired to search for clues concerning a long-lost daughter.

Admittedly wary when first approached and afraid of building her hopes too high, Olivia had learned that her mother had been married to Ira Carlisle for a number of years. When the marriage ended, Avis left without informing Ira that a third child was on the way. As a result, Olivia had grown up not knowing she had a father, and an older brother and sister. Finding out she had a family was a lifelong dream; and typically, the reality didn't live up to the fantasy.

When Ira died six months ago, Olivia had sincerely mourned the loss. He'd divided his beloved farm equally between his three grown children. Jared and Jessie had each received their generous portions when they married, so the terms of the will no longer governed their lives. But it created havoc with Olivia's life.

Leave it to Ira not to leave any loose ends—particularly concerning his long-lost daughter, Olivia thought with a dispirited sigh. In his ironclad will,

Ira left her a share of Stone's End, which included the original farmhouse and a fair parcel of land.

There was only one small catch. She needed a wedding certificate in order to claim it. The terms gave her a year to find a husband and tie the knot.

She had only six months left.

Olivia shifted the car into gear. A red warning light in the dashboard caught her attention; her gas tank was nearly empty.

Fortunately the gas station attached to the diner was still open. She filled up, then stocked up on a few snacks from a vending machine. A couple of candy bars and bottled water should tide her over until she got home.

Moments later, when she turned the car key in the ignition, nothing happened. Holding her breath, she tried again. When the engine roared to life, Olivia released a deep sigh of relief.

She wouldn't let herself think of the long lonely stretch of road ahead or the empty house waiting.

By now, the diner was flashing a Closed sign.

A couple of motorcycles roared past. Trucks pulled out, heading east, west, south, anywhere but north—her direction.

At the first crossroads, Olivia slowed when she observed a deep shadow on the edge of the road. A hitchhiker. The man's features were shadowed, but she instantly identified the tall wiry build. She should keep driving. But Drew Pierce had generously repaired her car and asked for nothing in return.

How could she leave him stranded in the rain?

The small powder-blue car slowed to a stop.

Drew groaned inwardly. He thought he'd seen the last of her. Olivia. Now here she was again. He kept walking, hoping she'd get the message and drive on.

No such luck.

The horn beeped once, twice. Her persistence simply amazed him. When she reached to open the door, heat rushed out of the car.

"Do you want a ride?" she asked, her voice casual, but friendly, with that soft feminine persuasive note that could probably melt an iceberg.

Drew wasn't totally immune.

For a moment, he searched his brain for any excuse, some glimmer of common sense that would keep him from accepting her invitation and getting further involved with her, this woman who made him ache just by looking at her.

He looked up and then down the highway, hoping for a reprieve, any sort of transportation that didn't come with a delicate blonde in the driver's seat. Unfortunately no one else was going his way. Just then, he felt the rain penetrate another layer of his clothes. Despite the chilling reminder of his present circumstances, he was still tempted to refuse her offer.

Then common sense came to his rescue.

Drew tossed his gear into the back seat. Avoiding Olivia DeAngelis wasn't worth getting a case of pneumonia. He hoped.

"Thanks," he muttered, folding his considerable length into the small passenger seat of her car. He couldn't resist an irritated, "Do you make a habit of picking up strange men?"

Her eyes widened. "But I know you."

He sighed. "Lady, you don't know the first thing about me."

"The waitress vouched for you."

Biting off a few choice words, Drew said, "She

never set eyes on me before I walked in there to-night.''

"But she knows your family."

Drew stared at her in disbelief. "And that does it for you?"

"Why not? Is there something wrong with them?"

"No, of course not," Drew muttered, refusing to be drawn into that sensitive topic. "But that isn't the point."

"Then, exactly what is?" She tilted her head. Definitely not an airhead, he decided. Sharp intelligence and stubborn determination gleamed in her gray eyes when she insisted, "You did me a favor when you repaired my car. I always pay my debts."

Always?

He wondered if that was true.

For a moment, the overhead light illuminated the interior of the car, flickering over her bright hair and fair skin. In that instant, every detail about her registered in his mind, like an indelible stamp that would linger long after she did.

His gaze drifted lower. At some point, she'd unzipped her black leather jacket. Underneath, she wore a white tailored shirt and a snug-fitting suede vest. The look might have been severe, except for the whimsical needlework, roses and primroses, embroidered along the front panels. The vest hugged her, drawing his attention to the slender curve of her waist, the faint shadow between her breasts.

Drew dragged his eyes away from that sweetness, taking in the fine pulse beating in her throat. Her eyes looked wide—and wary—not totally trusting. Apparently she wasn't as brave, or as bold, as she appeared on the surface.

That look of vulnerability melted his irritation.

The interior car light wavered, then blinked off, shutting out her image.

"Just drive," Drew said, trying to dismiss her.

But his senses were filled with her. He smelled chocolate, and apples, and Olivia—a floral scent he couldn't quite identify though it nagged at him, tantalizing, yet innocent and fresh. Soft music played on the radio, flutes and drums—no doubt meant to be soothing—but the rhythm and the rain threatened his last ounce of resistance.

He hadn't been this close to a woman in five years—and he didn't plan to start with a delicate blonde with a sweet smile and false bravado. She was obviously too young, early twenties, he guessed, and she made him feel every single one of his thirty-two years. He'd gone into prison a cocky young man and come out older. The gap between them was more than years and couldn't be breached.

An awkward silence fell between them, splitting the air with tension. They drove north, at times passing a town, a blur on the landscape. Long stretches of open farmland and deep dark forests that looked dense and forbidding at night whizzed by.

At an intersection, her voice startled him. "I forgot to ask—you are going to Henderson?"

"Yes."

"Are you staying long?"

So now they were going to make conversation. "Only a few days. That's it."

"Oh." After a couple more failed attempts at conversation, she subsided into silence.

Drew preferred that to expanding their acquaintance. A relationship—even a fleeting one—wasn't in the cards. Nevertheless, he was aware of her. A few miles later, when she visibly drooped, he noticed. "Why don't I take over?"

The offer surprised Olivia.

"Thank you. I could use a break," she said, grateful for his consideration. She was exhausted.

They traded places. Olivia slid along the seat, while Drew got out and went around to the driver's side. After adjusting the seat to accommodate his long legs, he shifted the car into gear.

Olivia reached for a blanket from the back seat, then wrapped it around her shoulders. She sighed. Her eyes felt scratchy. Yet she couldn't sleep. She dreaded going home alone.

Stone's End would seem empty, the rooms filled with everyday reminders of Ira. Like so many, her memories of him were bittersweet. Nothing in Olivia's life had ever been simple. From the first, Ira had seen past her flimsy defenses.

Through some hereditary alchemy, he'd recognized a certain trait in her and known how desperately she wanted to belong, how much she loved Stone's End and everyone there—long before she knew it herself. Over the last four years, she'd grown to love Ira Carlisle; she thought he loved her. But then, he left the will, and now she wasn't so sure.

Why did love always have conditions?

Why wasn't she ever enough?

Earlier that day, she'd consulted a lawyer who termed the situation "awkward," as if finding a husband to meet the terms of her father's will was nothing more than an easy stroll down the aisle with a besotted bridegroom. Olivia had seen what love could do, and undo. Far better to rely on herself. In any case, there was no groom in sight, besotted or otherwise.

She had every reason to avoid marriage. Her parents were divorced before she was born. Among her mother's many marriages, the one to Mike De-Angelis had been the most stable, but even that hadn't lasted long—just long enough for Mike to adopt Olivia when she was ten. He'd given her a sense of security for the first time in her life. Out of loyalty, she still used his name.

She stifled a yawn, regretting that she'd changed her mind about staying overnight in Bangor and canceled her hotel reservation. Only hours ago, she'd waved her brother, his wife and their four children off at the airport. They'd be back in mid-December at the end of the Cornell University semester. She was going to miss them!

Nevertheless, she'd urged Jared to go when he offered to cancel his plans to present a wildlife lecture series, part of a prestigious grant connected to his veterinary practice.

Jared was concerned about her. Before leaving, he'd asked her not to do anything rash to comply with Ira's will. Olivia had promised. Now she cast a guilty glance in her companion's direction, wondering—did Drew Pierce come under the heading of something rash? Thank goodness Jared wasn't here.

Shifting uneasily, Olivia stared out the window at the passing night. Although the foliage was still at its peak, a few bare limbs marked the passage of autumn, the coming of winter. At first sight, she'd fallen in love with Maine's unspoiled beauty. With more experience, she'd learned it could be daunting.

Just as the wind could steal your breath, the winter could steal your soul.

Despite that, she loved it with a fierceness she couldn't quite explain. Like Stone's End, it was in her blood. She frowned at the thought and tried to deny the intensity of her feelings. In her experience, opening up and caring that much about anything, or anyone, always invited emotional chaos.

Now, deliberately shutting out her companion, Olivia leaned her head back and closed her eyes, just for a minute.

Some time later, when the car stopped, she sat up abruptly. "Are we home?" One glance at Drew's grim expression told her something was wrong.

He turned to look at her, his dark gaze apologetic. "No such luck. It's the battery again."

Was this a recurring bad dream?

"But you fixed it." She twisted in her seat to stare at him. "It was working fine."

Drew released a harsh breath. "A temporary fix. You probably need a new battery."

"Where can we get one?" She looked out the window. They were in the middle of nowhere. "Where are we?"

"We just drove through Stillwater."

Suddenly aware that the temperature in the car had dropped several degrees, Olivia shivered. "We're still miles from Henderson."

He nodded, saying impatiently, "You're half-frozen. We can't stay here. I know a place nearby, a summer cabin."

She looked at him in dismay. "Do you think it's wise to go wandering around the forest in the dark?"

"It may be overgrown, but there used to be a path. I think I can find it."

At a glance, the woods looked thick and dark. Although her car had let her down, Olivia clung to the familiar safety. "But shouldn't we stay right here and wait for help?"

"Look, we can't stay here. I haven't seen another car on this road in over an hour. So you can forget about anyone coming to our rescue. That gives us two options."

Options—that didn't sound too awful. "What are they?"

"We can sit here and argue all night, with the temperature dropping below freezing, and risk hypothermia. Or we can go to this cabin. It's pretty basic, but we can get a fire going."

Aware that she was quickly running out of excuses not to venture out into the night, Olivia argued, "But if you haven't been there in a while, how do you know it's still standing?"

"It's sturdy, built of logs, and it's been around for more than fifty years. It's not going anywhere." His patience worn thin after the lengthy explanation, Drew climbed out of the car. "We can walk. It's not far."

After a moment's hesitation, she followed.

Drew knew his way around cars—fast cars and fast women. He had a bad feeling about this one— the car, not the woman. Or maybe both, if he was honest. In any case, he suspected there might be something seriously wrong with her car, something more complicated than a dead battery. The car had gradually lost power. He'd coaxed it up the last hill before it came to a dead stop. Now they were stuck.

He waited while Olivia tucked a few candy bars in her pocket, then reached for her purse and her umbrella. Juggling all three, she wrapped the wool blanket around her, then opened her umbrella. A strong gust of wind tore it out of her hand. It took off, twisting and twirling down the road, round and round, like a spinning top.

"Oh!" She tripped in her attempt to retrieve it.

"Leave it." Drew took her hand, surprised at how it fit.

They walked.

At least he was on familiar ground. There was a lake nearby, more cabins. Logging roads crisscrossed the area. He was familiar with those. Squinting into the darkness, he looked around for a landmark. His gaze fell on a break in the solid line of pine trees edging the road.

Locating a road overgrown with leafy ferns, he ducked under a branch, Olivia at his heels. Within the forest, tall pines provided some shelter from the rain. Everything smelled damp.

And fresh.

Washed new.

"This looks right," he said to assure her.

"It does?" Olivia peered into the dark gloomy woods.

He murmured back, "Mmm."

The wind carried a bite.

Left with little choice but to go where Drew led, Olivia plodded on through the thick brush. He obviously knew his way—as if he had an inner compass. Olivia stumbled, catching her breath when he caught her waist and righted her on the path. She didn't find her voice until he released her.

"Thanks," she murmured huskily.

"Watch your step." With that instruction, he moved on, obviously expecting her to follow in his wake.

"Me Tarzan, you Jane," she muttered under her breath.

She might have laughed, except that she didn't think he'd appreciate the joke. So far, she hadn't found any evidence of his having a sense of humor. He was outdoorsy and rugged—a handy man to have around under the circumstances. Trying to imagine some of her artsy friends back in San Francisco coping in a similar situation, she smiled.

He caught her expression and frowned. "What's so funny?"

Olivia gulped. "Nothing at all."

Clearly he didn't see any humor in their situation. When he looked at her like that, all dark-browed and glowering, she didn't, either. He turned back to the path, and she released a frustrated sigh. Make that outdoorsy, rugged and moody. She plodded on, pushing aside a branch.

It snapped.

The sound echoed through the night.

Olivia shivered.

The road was full of deep ruts. It went nowhere, except deeper into the woods. With each step, images of lurid newspaper headlines filled her imagination. It wasn't that she didn't trust him, it was just that…well, she wasn't a complete idiot.

She laughed nervously. "I should warn you my father was a cop in San Francisco. He taught me how to defend myself."

Drew grunted something unintelligible.

Despite the lack of response, she persisted. "He taught me how to use a gun."

"So you're armed and dangerous?"

Olivia stiffened at the challenge in his voice. "I don't carry a gun with me. But I do have a can of mace in my purse. And I have a black belt in karate. So don't try anything."

At that deliberate challenge, he stopped and turned to glance at her. "Is that supposed to frighten me?"

Olivia caught the cynical twist in his smile and regretted that she'd put it there. "Well, I wouldn't want to hurt you." She laughed, realizing he could probably recognize the fake note.

Unfortunately Drew didn't feel like laughing back. "You are really something." There was dry irony in his voice. He should have known Olivia DeAngelis was too good to be true.

All that sweet innocence and trust had disappeared at the first sign of trouble. He supposed he had to get used to that now that he had a prison record. As if matters couldn't get worse, her stepfather had been a cop!

He turned back to the path.

"I didn't mean to offend you," she said at his back after a moment of strained silence.

"You didn't." He smiled tightly. "In fact, it's a relief to know that if there's any trouble, you can defend yourself against all threats, even bears."

Her voice wavered, suddenly unsure.

"What bears?"

Drew laughed. "You never know. One might come along."

"You're just trying to frighten me." Despite the bravado, she picked up the pace, walking close to his back where the road narrowed into a single over-grown track. "There aren't really any bears, are there?"

"They rummage around these woods for food, both day and night. It doesn't help that the tourists feed them."

"Oh." Clearly alarmed, she pressed a hand to the candy bars in her pocket; she was a walking target.

"You needn't worry." He waited to hear her faint sigh of relief before he added, "Just stay close."

Olivia bit back a retort. If that was meant to be reassuring, it wasn't. In fact, given a choice, she didn't know who posed the biggest threat to her safety and peace of mind—Drew Pierce or a raven-ous bear, who might or might not have an appetite for her.

Drew stopped suddenly.

With her head down, Olivia walked right into his back. It felt solid, warm. She looked around his shoulder.

A cabin was visible in a clearing. At first glance, it looked abandoned. Built out of logs, it was rustic, long and low, and surprisingly large. There were No Trespassing signs posted all over the place.

Olivia frowned. "It's private property. We can't just break into the place."

Ignoring her, Drew found a key under the mat, then opened the door and entered. "I know the own-ers. They won't mind." At the evidence of recent use, he added, "Looks like someone's been using it as a hunting camp."

Once inside, Olivia took note of the sparse fur-nishings—a lopsided oak table and chairs, a sofa, plus two cots, one on each wall. She didn't dwell on the sleeping arrangements. A door to the left probably led to a kitchen. She hoped there was a bathroom.

Drew found an oil lamp and lit a match to it. The small light wavered, throwing the corners of the room in shadow.

Olivia asked, "Do you hunt?"

"I used to." Drew didn't explain that he'd stopped hunting years ago after he accidentally shot a neighbor's dog. The Carlisles had never forgiven him for that...and other things too numerous to mention.

The sight of Olivia still wrapped in her wool blanket brought him back to the present. She looked frozen. He raked out some leaves, then set some tinder and a few logs on the fireplace grate. He lit it with a match from a box that sat on the mantel, and soon had a fire blazing.

A neatly piled stack of wood stood beside the fireplace.

"That should see you through the next few hours," he said with satisfaction. "There's a generator housed in a shed out back, but I don't think you'll need it."

Olivia latched on to the one small detail he'd failed to explain. "Where are you going?"

"To see if I can dig up a mechanic. Stillwater's only a few miles back the way we came."

"But it's raining," she objected.

He headed for the door. "It's either that, or spend the night here."

Olivia's gaze skittered over the narrow cots. She backed away, wrapping the blanket tighter. "I'll be fine."

Nevertheless, she followed him out to the covered porch.

Since first setting eyes on Drew Pierce, she'd felt threatened; now she felt more alarmed by his imminent departure.

Perhaps sensing her unease, Drew looked back. "Don't go wandering around on your own in the dark. There's a lake nearby and some ledges."

"I won't." She didn't want to fall. Warning taken.

He smiled. "Then there are the bears."

She smiled back. "I've got my spray can of mace."

He laughed, sounding so masculine and sure. "I'll be back in a couple of hours."

She nodded.

Despite the urge to cling, Olivia let him go. Although she had no guarantee, she didn't think he'd leave her stranded. In fact, he'd probably send someone back to get her; but she didn't expect much more consideration from him. After all, he didn't owe her anything. She knew how easily people broke their promises.

Her less-than-ideal childhood had left Olivia wary and afraid to trust. She and her mother had lived in so many places, one step ahead of an eviction notice. Despite all the setbacks, large or small, Avis had always managed to bounce back. Olivia had recognized but never fully understood her mother's false air of gaiety until she was old enough to appreciate the cost of her mother's freedom.

Olivia was still paying the emotional price.

How many times had her mother left her small daughter at a friend's house while she took off with the latest man in her life? Olivia never knew when, or if, Avis would be back. For the most part, people had been kind. But sometimes, even the most generous of friends had grown impatient with being saddled with a child for long periods of time. Olivia had learned to read the signs when her welcome wore off.

Now as she watched Drew walk away and disappear into the gloomy night, she recalled all the other promises to come back that hadn't been kept. She had no intention of falling for a man's promises. She sighed. It was the perfect ending to a frustrating day.

Chapter Three

Drew didn't look back. The long walk into the nearest town cleared his head. Heaven knew, he needed it. Stillwater hadn't changed much, he noted. Built around a quaint town square, it was vintage New England.

A clear, crystal-blue lake provided recreational activities and drew tourists year-round. The fall foliage season was now in full swing, which meant that every hotel and motel within miles was probably filled to capacity. The town was all a bit too familiar.

Drew had misspent his youth here, then lived through more years than he cared to admit regretting that turbulent period. He'd grown up in the neighboring town of Henderson. At the age of eighteen, like a lot of restless teens, he'd thought his hometown was too small to hold him.

So he'd gone looking for some excitement in Stillwater, which was equally small, but the scenery was different, especially the girls. He'd found one girl he thought was special, but she'd proved him wrong. The scars from that experience had lingered a long time.

Now, through some stroke of misfortune, he was linked up with Olivia, who was clearly bad luck—as if he couldn't come up with enough of his own. It continued.

For one thing, the gas station was closed. But they had an emergency phone number. Drew dialed it on a pay phone and got quick results. A mechanic agreed to come out with a tow truck—just in case.

While Drew waited for the man to arrive, he leaned his shoulder against the phone booth. A short overhang sheltered him from the rain. His gaze wandered down Main Street, drawn to the Stillwater Inn. The place had a new front, new owners. But it was still rustic, overlooking the lake. The water lapped at the dock.

Long ago, he'd fallen in love with a waitress from the Stillwater Inn. They'd both been hotheaded, rebellious and far too young to handle their emotions. As a result, they'd argued, broken up and made up so many times that he lost count. And in between one of those times, Laurel slept with another guy.

But that wasn't the worst of it.

She'd tried to trap Drew into marriage by claiming the child she was expecting was his—instead of Jared Carlisle's. She'd died tragically young and left her twin sister, Rachel, to raise Dylan. Drew winced at the memory. Laurel had done more than damage his ego. The hell of it was, he might have given in to impulse and married her if she hadn't lied. In the end, his father paid her off. She'd wanted the Pierce money, not Drew.

At least he didn't have to worry about that anymore. For too long, he'd relied on his family's wealth and position. With it, he was nothing—a spoiled, arrogant young man. Without it, he didn't know who he was.

Fifteen minutes later, the repair truck pulled up to the curb. A mechanic called out, "You the guy with a breakdown?"

Drew smiled. He was close. "Yeah, that's me. I checked the car battery. It won't hold a charge."

"Well, let's go have a look. You coming?" he added when Drew didn't make a move toward the truck.

Drew wasn't sure of his next move. In all honesty, he was tempted to give the guy directions and be on his way, but the memory of a woman's resigned smile stopped him. Olivia had rightly guessed he was a loner; she probably thought he was a loser, as well. Under the circumstances, he couldn't argue either label, which should free him from obligation.

She obviously didn't expect him back. He didn't know why she didn't expect more from men, or from life. But for some reason, he wanted to prove her wrong, at least in this instance.

The mechanic said curtly, "You coming? I don't have all night." The man's impatience did it.

With a resigned sigh, Drew climbed into the truck. He didn't like the thought of Olivia dealing with the situation on her own. Face it, he felt protective. He frowned at the admission, not liking that at all. After today, he was never going to see her again. Until then, what was a few more hours of inconvenience?

"You're Drew Pierce," the mechanic said after they'd been driving awhile. His gaze remained fixed on the two-lane highway.

"Yes." Drew braced himself for the rest.

"I remember seeing your picture in the newspapers."

That wasn't surprising. The trial had been a three-ring circus. Instead of reacting to the man's open challenge, Drew raised a casual eyebrow. "That so?"

When Drew failed to react, the man backed down. "Yeah, well…guess it was long ago. Most folks have forgotten."

Drew doubted that very much. Small towns had long memories and even longer grudges. He had vivid memories of faces filled with hatred and contempt. The judge had thrown the book at Drew, giving him the maximum sentence. Well, he'd served his time. He wasn't about to defend himself all over again.

"That's the car." Drew spotted the small blue car, relieved to cut the subject short.

It didn't take long to install a new battery.

Drew turned the key in the ignition. Nothing.

With a shake of his head, the mechanic pronounced, "The car's in rough shape. It needs some other new parts." He listed just a few. "I can order them. Could take some time, though."

"It's not my car." Drew frowned as the awkwardness of the situation began to sink in. He didn't have money for repairs. In addition, he wasn't going anywhere that night. Neither was Olivia. They were stranded. "You can ask the owner."

The man frowned in confusion. "Fine with me. Where?"

"Back there." Drew nodded toward the rough logging road.

Fortunately, the tow truck had four-wheel drive. When they reached the camp, Drew was surprised to see the place softly lit. Smoke came from the chimney, and Olivia stood in the door.

Waiting.

"Hi." She smiled a warm greeting, all flushed-faced and sleepy-eyed, and Drew could feel himself falling, tumbling—

The mechanic broke the spell. "Looks like you got a cozy setup here." He was leering at Olivia.

Drew shoved his hands in his pockets. He wanted to hit the guy. Instead, he took a deep breath, admitting that the man's reaction was only natural. Olivia was a sight to behold. He couldn't deny his own gut response. Since the first moment he set eyes on her, he'd wanted to punch every man who looked at Olivia—which was pure insanity. Or something else. Whatever it was, he'd get over it.

The mechanic introduced himself. "Hi, I'm Walt."

Olivia smiled that megawatt smile. "How do you do, Walt?"

Now the mechanic had a name.

Drew liked him less and less.

The door opened wider.

Olivia hid her pleasure at Drew's return, instinctively protecting herself until she could control her response. Half-asleep, she'd heard the sound of an engine, at first surprised, then relieved to see Drew. Perhaps that was why her heart was racing. Despite all the inner alarm bells issuing a warning, she liked him.

And he was proving more dependable than a lot of men.

Could he be the solution to all her problems?

"Won't you come in?" She tried to focus her attention on the mechanic, deeply aware of Drew when he moved to stand near the fireplace, unbuttoning his jacket, then leaning his shoulder against the mantel. "Do you think you can fix my car, Walt?"

Entering the rustic cabin, Walt took off his hat. "That's what we have to talk about. I replaced the battery—that's part of the problem, but not all. I can get new parts, but it will take a day—or two."

"Are the parts expensive?"

Walt named his price, assuring her it was fair. "In the meantime, I can give you a lift to town. Don't know if you'll find a room, though. Things are pretty well booked up with tourists." He scratched his head. "Wish I could be more help."

Mentally calculating the cost of parts, plus labor, plus towing costs—the list kept growing—Olivia knew she could afford a motel room or car repairs, but not both.

"I suppose we could stay here." She glanced at Drew. "I mean, we are here. And there's no sense looking for a place for just one night, is there?" When he raised an eyebrow, she rushed on. "It's warm and dry." And free. "What do you think?"

Drew shrugged. "Guess that settles it."

Olivia smiled in relief. "Guess so."

For a moment, their gazes met, a head-on collision. Olivia flushed at the expression in his eyes. Odd how they could agree so completely, yet leave so many questions unanswered.

"Well, if you're sure," Walt said a moment later when he turned to leave.

"We're sure," Drew said dryly.

Walt gave Drew a lift back to the car to get his backpack and Olivia's one piece of luggage, which she'd brought in case she'd decided to stay overnight in Bangor. Drew couldn't help wishing she had— they might never have met.

After seeing Walt off, Drew walked back to the cabin, where he turned on the generator before going inside. He found Olivia asleep on one of the cots. She'd removed all but the white tailored shirt and set her clothes out to dry.

Wrapped in a blanket, cocooned, with her arms curled around a pillow, she looked so young. Pale shadows lined her eyes; she looked exhausted. Yet she'd never complained. Not once. Her insistence on looking at the bright side of the situation was almost comical. It was also touching.

Tearing his gaze away, Drew frowned, not liking the direction of his thoughts. He looked around the room. She'd found some sheets and a blanket and made up his cot. It looked narrow, meant for one, not all that inviting.

With a weary sigh, Drew took off his jacket, then stripped down before he dropped onto the cot. It felt lumpy and hard, but he'd slept on worse. He closed his eyes. A room, at least fifteen feet wide, separated him from Olivia.

A warm fire crackled in the grate. A log fell. Wind battered the small log building. Rain hit the metal roof. Then there was Olivia.

He could hear her breathing.

How the hell was he supposed to sleep?

Hours later the sun poured through the dusty windows.

Olivia awoke, disoriented at first, to find herself wrapped in her wool blanket, instead of her familiar quilt. Her face flushed with heat when her gaze landed on her roommate. Drew was asleep. He lay flat on his back. With the morning light pouring through the window, Olivia took in his broad shoulders, his broad muscled chest covered with coarse dark hair.

Black stubble covered his chin. His facial features were perfectly aligned, almost too beautiful for a man, except for the strength in his square jaw. In sleep he looked younger, more vulnerable, but his brow was wrinkled in a frown, as if his dreams brought him no peace.

Hastily Olivia looked away, aware that she'd invaded some private area. Somehow she knew he wouldn't appreciate the intrusion.

At the sight of her small overnight case on the table, Olivia rose, picked up the case and tiptoed from the room. The night before, she'd discovered a utilitarian bathroom. She flipped on a light switch, pleased to note that Drew must have turned on the generator, which meant there was hot water.

Olivia showered in the small metal cubicle, then dressed in the clothes she'd worn yesterday to impress her lawyer with her maturity. She needn't have bothered. He'd advised her to find a husband, adding, "A pretty little thing like you shouldn't have a problem.'' Like most men, he refused to look past the feminine package.

Admittedly she was guilty of using that package to her advantage on occasion, but she had no respect for men she could manipulate, which was one more reason to appreciate Drew Pierce. She knew he was attracted to her, but he seemed equally determined not to do act on it. Olivia slowly buttoned her shirt.

She couldn't deny the obvious—Drew Pierce could be the solution to all her problems. Since he was ''just passing through'' as he put it, she wondered if he'd be willing to stick around Henderson long enough to attach his name to a marriage certificate.

There was no provision in the will stating they had to live together. In six months the marriage could be annulled. No strings and no one would get hurt.

She wondered if Drew could be bought, then recoiled at the idea of even asking him to marry her. But what if? What if she asked and what if he said yes? She trembled. Would she be willing to pay the price?

In her heart, the part of her that always remained carefully guarded, Olivia knew that marriage should be a permanent bond, but things didn't always work out as they should.

From what she knew about Drew's past, she doubted if he had many romantic illusions that might get in the way, or many scruples, for that matter. But then, what did she know about him? His critics were harsh, but she sensed there was more to him than gossip revealed.

Perhaps it was unwise, but she couldn't deny that something in Drew aroused her sympathy. Her step-

father had been a cop. She'd had enough exposure
to the criminal justice system to know that it broke
some men. She wondered how Drew had survived it.
Had it left him hurt and wounded in some way? Did
that account for his long silences, his lack of
warmth?

Olivia turned away, uncomfortable with the
thought, and headed into the kitchen. She reached for
a pot and started to hum....

Drew awoke abruptly.

He wasn't sure what had disturbed him. But his
first thought was that this was day four. His fourth
day of freedom! With his eyes closed, he could hear
the blessed sound of silence. It was interrupted by
the sound of a woman's soft humming.

Drew frowned, recalling his present situation—all
the inconveniences, delays and disruptions—and
they all had to do with Olivia DeAngelis. He could
hear her puttering around the kitchen, opening cup-
boards, rattling pots and pans. When a teakettle whis-
tled, he almost jumped out of his skin.

With a groan, Drew pulled on a pair of jeans and
a shirt. Not in the mood to face Olivia's early-
morning chirpiness, he slipped out the front door.

The storm had cleared the air. The air was cool
and crisp and dry. The breeze felt good. Drew raised
his gaze to the treetops scraping a brilliant blue sky.
The sun filtered through, setting the maple leaves on
fire. Nature's celebration.

But autumn was all illusion, a time when nature
signaled the end of a green growing season with
bright gaudy displays of color, a time when life
seemed exaggerated and desperate. As each day narrowed, there were clear signs that winter was on its

way. It could be beautiful, but brutal, if you were unprepared...if you were alone. And Drew had forfeited every close tie.

Olivia interrupted his downward mood. "Good morning." She'd come outside bearing gifts—a steaming mug of coffee.

"Morning," he said, taking her in at a glance. A calf-length green skirt had replaced her tight black jeans—which was a relief. But when she moved, the skirt "swished" and he was lost again, enchanted by her intrinsic femininity. The coffee was strong. He took a bracing swallow.

"Do you need sugar?"

"No." His voice sounded husky.

She smiled. "That's just as well. There isn't any. Apart from that," she said, as if he had a burning desire to know each domestic detail, "the kitchen's pretty well stocked. I found some coffee and powdered milk."

He lifted his cup. "So I see."

"There are some canned goods. I checked the expiration dates and they're all safe. I was going to make pancakes for breakfast, but there aren't any eggs. There is such a thing as powdered eggs, but I suppose that would be expecting too much." She laughed, her eyes bright and alive. *She* was so alive. "How do you feel about canned hash or baked beans for breakfast?"

More choices.

Drew took another gulp of coffee. "Hash sounds good."

"Tuna casserole for lunch?"

He nodded, but didn't dare ask what went into that besides the tuna. She continued to chatter.

When she ran out of menu items, she started on Drew. "So what do you do—for work, I mean?"

He said dryly, "Let's just say I'm between jobs at the moment." Had he actually ever held down a real job, one that wasn't manufactured for him, one that he cared about?

Olivia chuckled. "Any particular field?"

He shrugged. "Not really." He had a college degree in forestry gathering dust somewhere, not that it amounted to much. "How about you? What do you do?"

Unconsciously provocative, with the breeze playing with the hem of her skirt, she stared at him with her wide-spaced gray eyes. Her eyelashes were long and lush, fanning her flushed cheeks. "I'm a hooker."

Drew choked on his coffee, gulping in air when he finally recovered his voice. "What did you say?"

Clearly pleased to have captured his full attention, she repeated, "I'm a hooker. I hook rugs. You know, cut and dyed, originally designed, handcrafted wool rugs?" She laughed at his expression. "I have an art degree, which doesn't earn much in this part of Maine. I'm not cut out for the starving artist-in-a-garret route, so I had to find something practical to do. I do all kinds of needlecrafts, as well."

"And that pays the bills?"

"Yes." A mischievous dimple played around her pursed mouth. "I'm sorry, I didn't mean to shock you." The little witch didn't look sorry at all; in fact, she looked downright smug.

"You didn't shock me," he said, trying not to laugh.

Her gray eyes twinkled. "Oh, yes, I did."

He considered kissing that sassy mouth, then thought better of it. "You do know that kind of talk could land you in a hell of a lot of trouble in certain circles."

The fact that she felt safe with him had registered.

She shrugged. "It's only a joke. Most people think it's pretty funny."

His gaze ran over her, every delectable inch. He shook his head, marveling at her innocence. "You're lucky it was me. Not one of those guys at that diner last night."

Olivia didn't feel lucky. In fact, she felt odd, and her pulse had quickened with the sweep of his dark eyes.

"I'm sorry," she murmured, wondering why she was apologizing. Maybe the joke was on her. She'd felt his scorching glance—which only made her more aware of his maleness...and her helpless response.

But at least he was smiling!

Flustered, Olivia looked past him to the surrounding forest. "It's so beautiful out here. Have you ever seen a tree with leaves that shade of banana gold?" she asked, knowing she sounded like a tourist. "What is it?"

He chuckled. "That's a birch tree. Where did you live in California?" He leaned against the porch rail, looking at her.

Under that lingering gaze, Olivia felt herself flushing. "I grew up in lots of places before winding up in San Francisco." She smiled, unaware that it was wistful, remembering the frequent moves and upheavals of her childhood. Her mother was always looking for something better than what she had, something different. Many times, Olivia had felt like the grown-up.

"Do you have family in California?" he asked.

"There's no one close." She shook her head. "Not anymore. How about your family?"

Drew looked away. "They're scattered around. We don't stay in touch." He knew it was the perfect opening. He should tell her about his situation.

Part of him wished she knew about his past, and part of him dreaded her finding out, especially from someone else. He should tell her. When he didn't add any details, she turned toward the house.

"Well, I should do something about a meal," she said. And suddenly he wanted to call her back.

But the moment passed.

After breakfast, Drew felt restless, confined. He decided to go for a walk, just because he could.

When informed of his plan, Olivia tilted her head. "That sounds like fun. Mind if I join you?"

Drew hid his irritation. "Sure." He didn't know how to stop her—short of locking her in the cabin— or telling her she couldn't come. And somehow he couldn't do either.

He grabbed his denim jacket, then waited while she took a jacket from her case. She pulled it on, tugging at the sleeve. The jacket was a tapestry of richly colored floral embroidery.

He recognized her unique touch. "Did you make that?"

She nodded, "Mmm." Obviously a girl of many talents.

Outside, a breeze caught her hair. Bright leaves fell all around, carpeting the ground in colors of red, gold and russet. The crunch of dry leaves under

Drew's feet felt familiar. As a youth, he'd felt a special affinity for the woods. As he grew older, he'd forgotten that—just one of the things he'd taken for granted and ignored when it was his for the taking. Perhaps in his arrogance, a man could only appreciate the things that were hard-won. He took a deep breath, inhaling the scent of pine and woods.

They followed a path down to the crystal-clear lake. With Olivia tagging along, Drew soon realized that a silent communion with nature wasn't in the cards. She was full of information.

Her chatter irritated him at first; but then the gentle rhythm of feminine tones soothed a loneliness he'd never acknowledged. A deep well that had never been filled. The realization startled him. He'd never thought of a woman as a companion. A soul mate. Perhaps if he had, he might have had better luck finding one.

She sighed, drawing his attention back. She was a feast for the eyes—eyes that had only seen drab concrete walls for so long. Like spun gold, yellow birch leaves fluttered down around her. "I was hoping to see some wildlife," she said.

He chuckled. "Hush, you're scaring them all away." He placed his hands on her shoulders, then turned her toward the water's edge. "Just wait a few minutes, then you'll see."

She leaned back slightly, and Drew caught his breath at the brush of her skirt against his thigh.

As predicted, before long, a doe with her fawn appeared, taking dainty steps out of the woods. They stopped by the water, dipping their heads to drink. Under his hands, Olivia stood absolutely still—until the doe prodded her offspring back up the steep bank and into the woods.

"How absolutely beautiful," she whispered.

She turned, standing close. Her breasts were a tantalizing inch from his chest. All it took was one deep breath. At the physical contact, her lips parted on a small gasp.

"Olivia," he murmured her name. Like a starving man, he wanted to drag her close and kiss her—taste her—but he knew he wouldn't stop there.

Slowly releasing her, he stepped back.

Revealing her confusion, her hand shook as she brushed her hair back from her face. "Drew?"

He shook his head, saying harshly, "Nothing. Forget it."

Without further word, he turned and walked away.

Even if tempted, he had nothing to offer a woman like Olivia. Except himself. And that was never enough for the women he'd known in the past.

They had nowhere to go but back to the cabin. Once fully aroused, he dreaded spending another night alone with Olivia.

Before meeting her, he'd had a plan—go to Henderson, pick up his car, cash out a small trust fund and pick up some clothes. He planned to grab his possessions and go somewhere—he didn't know where. A woman, no matter how tempting, was no reason to change his plan.

After a moment, Olivia caught up with him. She was silent—now that she'd succeeded in twisting him in knots.

A winding lakeside path took them to the road. About a mile downhill from the camp, they passed a farmer's market and stopped to buy fresh eggs and milk. Fresh poultry. Some tomatoes. Apples. Drew took out his wallet to pay.

Olivia kept adding items.

Finally she walked toward him with a bouquet of flowers, ruffled hollyhocks in pink, red and purple mixed with lacy-edged white and yellow mums, clutched in her hand.

At the sight of her, Drew felt his chest squeeze. For a moment, he couldn't breathe. There hadn't been many flowers in his life lately. And maybe that was what was missing.

Along with a few other things.

With a knowing smile, the farmer's wife accepted his money and commented, "Your girl is very sweet."

Your girl.

Olivia reached him. "I couldn't resist the flowers. You don't mind, do you?"

Mind?

No, in fact, he loved it. At the admission, Drew felt his heart twist like a leaf in the wind...falling. If only their situations were different. If only life would give him a second chance. If only he hadn't messed up every good thing in his life.

Her face animated with pleasure, Olivia lifted the brilliantly colored flowers to her dainty nose. "They smell delicious."

"Yes, they do." Drew smiled back. She'd spent his last dollar on a bunch of flowers. He was down to an uncashed check from his sister and he didn't care!

Hell!

He must be going soft, getting all sentimental

about a woman he'd known less than twenty-four hours—a woman with laughter in her voice, sunshine in her eyes, pale flyaway hair and a come-hither smile that beckoned him to discover her secrets.

Chapter Four

Drew's smile grew ironic. Oh, he knew he was susceptible, feeling deprived and vulnerable to anything in a skirt. He'd vowed not to seduce the first woman he came across, not even the second or the third.

With one bewitching smile, Olivia made it hard to remember exactly why he'd made such a stupid, impractical vow. She was there to tempt, to tease, to test him. Women had always come so easily, perhaps too easily. No matter how he tried to deny it, he couldn't help but wonder—would she?

They were going to be alone for another night. He had no idea how he was going to keep his hands off her. He laughed without humor. The gods must be having a field day.

It was payback time for every indiscretion he'd ever committed—and there was a long string of them. Drew could only assume Olivia was going to drive him crazy for the next twenty-four hours, if he held out that long.

"Let's head back." He wished he had an alternative choice, some place to go, but he didn't.

She checked the items she'd purchased. "I think we've got everything." She waved to the farmer's wife, who insisted on giving Olivia some fresh cream from the dairy.

"You'll need some to top off that apple cobbler," the woman insisted.

Apparently Olivia planned to do some baking. Drew marveled at her easy adaptability.

Olivia waved farewell to her new friend—she obviously had a knack for collecting them—and fell into step beside him. She was so small, reaching only up to his shirt collar. Her step was light, graceful.

All the way back to the cabin, Olivia stuck close to his side—less than a foot away. He felt dizzy from the scent of flowers. More than once, he regretted teasing her about hungry bears. Now he had to endure her nearness.

Then there was her soft voice, the bounce in her step, the gleam in her smile, the soft accidental brush of her hand against his—all guaranteed to wear down his resistance.

Was it all innocent?

Or was it only wishful thinking on his part?

They walked back to the cabin along the same track they'd found the day before. The woods were thick, endless, stretching in every direction. It would be easy to get lost in them.

The cabin greeted them like an old friend.

Built of roughhewn logs, weathered and burnished

to a soft gray, it glowed in the midday sun. The sunny glen seemed far from the immediate past.

And the future.

He had today. All anyone had really. Who knew what tomorrow would bring? He smiled wryly, admitting that Olivia's optimism was beginning to rub off on him.

She made lunch.

Either he was starving, or it was the best tuna casserole he'd ever eaten. Chin in hand, with her elbow leaning against the edge of the table, Olivia inched the serving dish closer.

"There's more," she offered.

Recognizing that enticing feminine note, Drew pushed away from the table and stood. "No, thank you."

It would take more than a combination of canned tuna, condensed mushroom soup and noodles to seduce him.

He grabbed for an escape hatch. "The farmer's wife took quite a shine to you. I'm sure she'd let you stay the night."

At the suggestion, Olivia shook her head. "But I don't know her. I can't just intrude. Besides, I'm comfortable here."

Drew had only known Olivia for one day—it felt longer—but he recognized that stubborn tilt to her chin. Knowing he was fighting a losing battle, he persisted. "Hasn't it occurred to you by now that you shouldn't trust me?"

She smiled at him. "But I do trust you. If you intended me any harm, you'd have done something about it by now."

"Not necessarily."

"Well, you've left behind a trail of witnesses, starting back at the diner. Then there's Walt, and the farmer's wife."

"Spoken like a true cop's daughter," he said with an edge, frustrated at his inability to simply walk away from her.

Shrugging off his bad humor, Olivia started to gather the dishes. "So what are we going to do with the rest of the day?"

We?

Drew raised an eyebrow. "Not bored already, are you?"

"Not exactly, but I like to keep busy. I wish I'd brought some needlework with me. I never expected this kind of delay."

She looked around. "This place could use a good cleaning."

"Why bother?" As usual, the feminine mind was a mystery.

"I could start on the windows—after the dishes, of course."

With a smooth move, she shoved a stack of plates, cups and saucers at him. "What's this?" he asked.

"Dishes. You wash and I'll dry," she said.

"Right." He looked down at the messy collection. He'd never washed a dish in his life!

At his hesitation, Olivia frowned. "That is, unless you'd rather dry?"

Drew gritted his teeth. "No, that's fine. I'll wash."

How hard could it be?

Fifteen minutes later, Drew stood with his arms up to the elbows in soapsuds. The sink overflowed. He frowned, wondering what had gone wrong.

Olivia mopped the floor. "You only need a capful of detergent."

The kitchen was small and didn't allow much room. Her hip brushing against his, she squeezed past him in the narrow space to reach a puddle of soap-suds by his foot.

Hiding his instant response to her nearness, Drew laughed huskily. "Now you tell me!"

"Never mind, the floor needed to be scrubbed, anyway."

Drew managed to finish the dishes while Olivia rinsed and dried. She was very efficient—so efficient that she went straight to washing the windows. But first, she changed into her black jeans. Yes, they fit exactly the way he remembered—snug.

Needing an escape, Drew decided it was time to chop some wood for the fireplace. Despite the day's warmth, he knew the night would turn cold. Besides, he needed to stay occupied.

For five years, he'd survived the loss of freedom by learning to focus on each moment, filling in time with assigned duties—eating, reading, watching television, working out and even sleeping on schedule.

Emotions had played no part in his life; but meeting Olivia had reawakened certain masculine needs. He couldn't deny that he wanted Olivia badly. He wished he could go back to a simple case of lust at first sight. Now, after spending just one day with her, Olivia had a personality, a mind and a heart to go with the perfection of her body.

Outside, he found the woodpile and a stack of sawed-off logs. Drew bent to his task. He set a split chunk of wood on end, then split it in halves, then fourths.

Then he reached for another, and another...

He'd been at it quite a while by the time Olivia came outside. She waved—he pretended not to notice. A moment later, he almost cut off his left foot when she climbed a stepladder and leaned forward to get at a stubborn spot on a pane of glass.

When he swore under his breath, she turned to look at him.

"Did you say something?" she asked.

"Nothing," he muttered, then went back to splitting logs. The woodpile grew...and grew.

After a while, apparently satisfied with the sparkling glass panes, Olivia came and sat on a log—close, but not too close.

Drew tried to ignore her. Fat chance.

She was looking at him as if she was measuring him for a suit—or a bed. Drew slammed the door on the thought.

He whacked another section of a log with the ax. He put all his strength in it, feeling a measure of satisfaction when the blade sliced through cleanly.

Olivia picked up a twig of pine brush, feathering and twirling it between her fingers, as she contemplated him with obvious curiosity.

"Did you grow up in Maine?" she asked after keeping him guessing about her next move.

"Yes," Drew replied with caution. He'd been fooled by her casual air before.

"You're very fortunate."

He quirked an eyebrow. "What makes you say that?"

"Well, I mean, look around you."

Frowning, he looked around and saw only trees. "I guess."

"You had all this freedom. All this space." Olivia spread her arms wide to encompass the surrounding forest. "No traffic jams, no smog."

"Just bad weather and bears," he said dryly.

She smiled. "Believe it or not, California has a few bears. And as far as bad weather goes, snow at least comes with a warning, not like an earthquake, which just happens."

"Good point."

She continued, "In Henderson, people don't even bother to lock their doors. I grew up in a neighborhood where being safe meant three sets of locks on the door."

"That must have been rough," he said, trying to imagine what her childhood must have been like.

"You probably never had to worry about a thief who sneaks up a dark stairwell. Or a random shooter seeking a thrill, or some teenage kids holding up a convenience store, then stealing a getaway car just for kicks." Her voice trembled. "My stepfather was a cop. One day, he was on routine duty. There was a robbery—a high-speed chase. He was killed when his cruiser crashed." She stopped abruptly, then took a deep breath before continuing. "I don't know why I said all that. I never talk about him."

"Maybe you should," Drew said, confounded when he realized what he'd invited. He didn't want her to confide in him, but it was too late to stop her now.

With a sad resigned smile, she said, "Talking about it doesn't change anything. He was a good cop, and he loved his job. From the time I was old enough to read the newspaper, I was afraid something like that might happen."

Olivia hadn't meant to reveal anything that personal to a stranger. But he was eyeing her with such sympathy and she was surprised at how badly she ached to tell someone about Mike—his generosity, his strength, his kindness. She swallowed.

"Olivia," he said softly, as if he could dam the hurt inside her. No one could repair her childhood. "I'm sorry. Your stepfather sounds like a good guy."

"Thanks." Olivia squared her shoulders. "I'm okay. It was all so long ago." She stood, then brushed the seat of her pants. "Anyway, thanks for listening." She kept her voice carefully neutral.

Moments later, Drew watched her walk away, aware that she'd broken through another barrier of his indifference.

In autumn, daylight spent itself early.

When the sun started to sink, the temperature dropped along with it. Drew gathered a few chunks of wood. He wasn't looking forward to a long cozy evening alone with Olivia.

He walked into the cabin. His face fell at the sight of the table set for two. Olivia had arranged the flowers in the center, next to a squat candle. Drew set the firewood on the pile beside the fireplace, then added a log to the flames.

"I thought we'd save the generator," she explained, lighting the candle.

"Good thinking." Drew joined her at the table.

"I hope you're hungry." She ladled a thick, creamy tomato-based soup into a bowl, then passed it to him. "I found a deck of cards—I thought we could have a game later. I'm a pretty good poker player."

Drew could well imagine—she had him going around in circles. He could think of only one way he wanted to fill the evening hours, and it wasn't playing two-man poker.

Fried chicken and corn on the cob, followed by apple cobbler made up the remainder of the meal. Drew ate more than his share. After dinner, they did the dishes, then played cards.

He lost.

"I win," she said, fanning out her cards to reveal three jacks and two queens—a full house.

Revealing two pairs, he chuckled. "I let you win."

"I hate a sore loser." Hiding a grin, she covered her mouth with the back of her hand and yawned delicately. "I'm exhausted. Do you mind if I use the shower first?"

He shrugged. "I'm not in any hurry."

With a half smile, he watched her disappear into the bathroom. Here he was, stranded overnight with a beautiful sexy woman—a woman who claimed she trusted him. Very clever. She tempted him, tied him up in knots, then did the old trust routine. And damned if it wasn't working. He couldn't seduce her—not unless she made the first move, and then all bets were off.

Half an hour later, Olivia came out of the bathroom wearing a thick fleece nightshirt. It was cuddly-looking, pale gray, and reached from her chin to her toes, but nothing could disguise the feminine curves beneath. Her hair was still damp, curling around her ears and throat.

"Your turn." She ran a brush through her hair.

His mind filled with the image of her, Drew

walked into the bathroom. It was still warm, still fragrant with the scent of her shampoo.

"Be careful…" Her warning came too late.

He walked into a makeshift clothesline strung across the small bathroom. It caught him squarely across the throat.

Next a damp silk shirt slapped him in the face. His startled gaze took in the tantalizing sight of black silk briefs and a matching lacy bra. It wasn't padded, he noted in the brief second it took him to tangle himself in it.

From behind, Olivia crashed into him. The floor was damp. He turned to catch her before she fell. With an "oomph," she landed against his chest. At the impact, he could feel himself slipping, sliding, falling.

With his hands tightening around her slender waist, he landed them both in the bathroom sink; his hip collided with the cold water tap, and water gushed out. Pressure forced it in all directions. Within seconds, he was drenched.

Olivia's face glistened with drops of moisture. "Sorry, did I forget to warn you—I rinsed out a few things earlier?"

Instead of an apology, laughter lit her eyes.

It was too much.

Drew dipped his head. He watched her soft gray eyes darken and widen with awareness seconds before his lips touched hers.

His hands spanned her waist as he dragged her closer, crushing her against his chest in a convulsive move. His needs were urgent, with no room for hesitation. When she didn't push him away, he coaxed her mouth open, then invaded, groaning when he felt the tip of her tongue.

His hands roamed over her, feeling warmth through the thick fleece fabric she wore. He wanted flesh on flesh. And she was wearing too many clothes, and so was he, and they were both drenched from the gushing faucet.

He reached back and turned it off.

Not breaking contact with her mouth, he lifted her slight weight and carried her into the main room. The flickering firelight guided him to his cot, where he gently lowered her, then settled beside her. The bed was narrow, but it would do.

He raised his head long enough to draw breath. With a faint smile, he smoothed pale hair from her flushed cheeks. Her hair was like silk, her skin rose-petal smooth.

He edged the collar of her nightshirt from her throat. "How do we get you out of this?"

She gulped, stiffening beneath him. "What?"

He groaned. "Please tell me you're not a virgin."

Her face reddened.

"You are." His eyes narrowed. He waited for her to deny it.

She didn't. Instead, she apologized. "I'm sorry, I thought you knew."

His voice deepened. "How the hell am I supposed to know?"

"I thought men just did."

"Well, we don't! I'm not a mind reader. So next time, don't go leading a man on unless you mean it."

Next time.

He lifted himself off the cot; he was halfway

across the room before he heard her soft voice.
"Drew, I'm sorry."

He fought the urge to go back and finish what he'd
started. His body felt tight with needs that hadn't
been met. He was so aroused, he felt as if the top of
his head was going to blow off.

But there was that entreaty in her voice.

With a deep sigh, he turned back. She sat in the
middle of his narrow bed; she looked young and
helpless.

And irresistible.

At some point, her nightshirt had ridden up. One
slender bare leg dangled over the edge of the bed.
Like the rest of her, her foot was small and dainty;
it didn't reach the floor. She was all slender and gold
and feminine. The little witch was going to drive him
insane.

His voice sounded harsh when he spoke. "I'm not
a eunuch or a saint—so let's get a few things straight.
From now on, you stay on your side of the room."

"Which side is mine?" Her gaze followed the direction of his hand as he defined her space—notably
separate from his.

He said firmly, "And I'll stay on mine."

Amused, her gaze came back to him. "That's ridiculous."

Drew looked at her. In his mind, all he saw was
an image of a black lace bra with pale round breasts
spilling out.

He added, "And no more lingerie in the bathroom."

"Oh." Finally she got it.

He released a long breath in relief. Maybe now,

with Olivia sufficiently warned to stay out of his way, they could both get some sleep.

Olivia felt very small, very naive; she cringed at the impatient note in his voice. Trying to evade his penetrating stare, she reached for a pillow and hugged it to her chest.

Their little encounter had obviously left him in a foul mood. Men were like that when they were frustrated—or so she'd been told. She'd never let one get close enough to find out.

In any case, he was obviously annoyed. And all over a little kiss—well, maybe not so little. Her mouth tingled from the contact, and her body felt empty, yet more alive. He'd clearly wanted her. She frowned at the realization that she'd wanted him back—which wasn't part of her plan.

What was her plan?

Oh, yes, she'd hoped to propose a temporary marriage over dinner. But the food had gotten in the way. Then he'd let her win at poker, which annoyed her.

She didn't know how to approach the subject of marriage. Surely, if she explained her situation, he'd see the mutual benefits of such an arrangement. Instead of the small allotment from a trust account she was getting now, she'd get full rights to Stone's End and access to a hefty bank account.

Although it struck her as mercenary, she could pay Drew for his time if that was what he wanted. How much was a husband worth in monetary terms?

She could afford to be generous—he certainly looked as if he could use the money.

All evening she'd been trying to soften him up, but her plans had gone astray, and so had she. Almost. She flushed at how she'd responded to him.

She'd had plenty of boyfriends, but Drew wasn't a boy. Her spirits sank. Now he was looking at her as if he didn't even like her!

Before she could find her voice, he muttered, "I never should have touched you."

She sighed, unsure what she wanted—just that she didn't want whatever had happened between them to end like this.

"I touched you first," she said, shifting on the bed.

"Stop right there." He held up his hand. "This is insane." He backed away. "Look, just stay away from me—unless you want to wind up sharing a bed tonight. You got that?"

"All right," she said slowly, shivering inside at the ravenous look in his eyes that seemed to drink her up and swallow her whole. She knew this man could hurt her—unless she could keep her emotions from interfering with what she needed to do.

She knew he had problems, but she couldn't get involved. She had enough problems of her own. "Drew, I—"

"There's no more to say," he said hoarsely.

"I was just wondering…" She pulled her damp nightshirt away from her skin. "Do you have something I could borrow to sleep in just for tonight?"

With a tight nod, he dug a plaid flannel shirt out of his backpack, then tossed it to her. Olivia caught it.

"Thanks," she murmured, deciding this wasn't the best time to pursue the topic of marriage.

However, one very large question loomed in her mind. Was Drew eligible? He didn't behave like a married man, but that didn't necessarily mean he was unattached. She typically dated men who were more comfortable—not exactly weak, but tame. Drew definitely had a dangerous edge. The urge to be the woman to domesticate him was almost irresistible. Had some woman tried?

Drew slammed into the bathroom.

He was breathing hard, as if he'd been running.

He stripped off his damp clothes and took a quick shower. The bathroom reeked of her shampoo and body powder. Subtle and fragrant, it was sophisticated yet innocent, sweet but sassy—like her. His stomach knotted at the scent. Later, when he climbed into bed, it was there, as well.

The full moon lit the room. He lay staring at the beamed ceiling. The wind whined to come in, seeking out every nook and crevice. Something scratched at a window—probably a branch.

He hoped.

He was in no mood for fighting off predators, whether they were two-legged or walked on all fours.

"Drew?" she whispered into the dividing space.

Inwardly he groaned. "What now?"

"I'm sorry."

"Let's drop it."

"Umm...I was just wondering...are you married?"

"No!" he said hoarsely. God, what was she up to now!

For several minutes, he waited for her to add more. When she didn't, he turned to look at her bright head against the white pillow. Her eyes were closed. She was breathing evenly.

She was asleep!

Hell, how was he supposed to sleep now? He

punched his pillow and turned on his side to stare at the rough wall.

For the second night in a row, Drew didn't get much rest.

The following morning, Olivia was still wearing his shirt.

Naturally it looked better on her than on him.

She'd tucked the red-and-black buffalo plaid into her black jeans. He knew he'd never wear the shirt again without recalling her in it. His gaze followed her hungrily as she set the food on the table. In silence, they ate breakfast—blueberry pancakes.

Like a starved man, Drew ate every crumb.

Olivia smiled at him, all rosy and innocent, as if he'd never invaded her mouth, never felt her breasts flatten against him. When she piled another pancake on his plate, he didn't refuse. Despite his lingering frustration, he had to admit she knew how to cook.

When the sound of an engine roared up the rough track and stopped just outside the door, Drew met Olivia's gaze. "That must be Walt."

"Mmm." She looked disappointed when he'd expected her to be overjoyed and anxious to get her car repaired and on her way.

A moment later, Drew opened the door and found Walt on the doorstep. Drew was never more pleased to see anyone in his life!

With a grin, Walt removed his baseball cap. "Morning. Your car's ready, almost good as new. It's back at the shop. Thought I'd give you a ride into town. Hope I'm not too early."

"Not at all," Drew said, noting with dry amusement the improvement in the man's appearance.

Walt had combed his hair and cleaned the grease from under his fingernails. Apparently Olivia had that sort of effect on people—particularly the male variety.

Olivia smiled, which probably earned her a hefty auto repair discount. "Would you care for some breakfast?"

"No, thanks." Walt took an empty chair at the table. "I just ate. Though I could use a cup of coffee if you got some."

At Olivia's urging, Walt had two cups of coffee and put away an impressive stack of pancakes.

Meanwhile, Drew gathered up his things and tended the fire, dousing it with a bucket of water to ensure it was out. Olivia tidied up the kitchen. Before leaving, Drew found her writing out an IOU with a meticulous list of what they'd used. An honest woman! With a faint smile, he recalled her claim that she always paid her debts.

"I'll take care of it." He took the note, without mentioning that his family owned the place.

The cabin was filled with memories of happier days spent with his parents, his two brothers and his sister. He could still recall racing his brothers down to the lake, then diving off the pier into the frigid waters. As a boy, he'd thought those summer days would never end. But they had.

Olivia looked around. "I guess that's it." She looked at Drew expectantly.

"Guess so." Drew might have added something, but Walt was waiting, and besides, what was there to say?

Fate had given him a stolen day and two nights, time out of time, with Olivia, a stranger who somehow felt more familiar than many people he'd known all his life. And somehow, she'd made the adjustment of going home to Henderson and facing his old life seem just a bit easier today than it had yesterday.

Olivia slipped her arms into her black leather jacket.

Walt tripped all over himself offering to carry her one small piece of luggage. He rushed to open the door for her.

Left behind, Drew took one last look around. The windows sparkled, the floor was swept clean, the scent of fresh flowers lingered.

Drew filed it away with all the other memories of this place. Olivia had left her mark.

Chapter Five

After the excitement of the past two days, reaching Henderson felt anticlimactic. Olivia tried to deny the reaction. Main Street wasn't much more than a short business strip. A few retail stores were boarded up.

In the town square, a bright profusion of red and gold chrysanthemums spilled out of a cultivated plot surrounding a stone monument commemorating some long-forgotten military hero who had fought in some long-forgotten battle.

This was where she and Drew would go their separate ways. Olivia hated goodbyes. The inevitable sense of loss was nothing new; but something about Drew touched her.

She couldn't deny a sinking sensation when he said, "You can drop me off anywhere here in town."

Of course, she'd already decided he wasn't the right man for her purposes. So why was she feeling dispirited? She should be relieved. Drew would probably have laughed at her marriage proposal. At least, she'd been spared that humiliation.

She slowed the car. ''Where?''

He shrugged. ''Here will do.''

Olivia pulled her car into a vacant spot in front of the Trading Post. A pair of moose antlers curved over the entrance. She turned to Drew, intending to say goodbye.

Instead, she heard herself saying, ''Maybe we could have dinner before you leave town.'' She wasn't in the habit of asking men for dates. This was a first.

His mouth tightened. ''Olivia, you don't want to know me. Not if you want to get along with people in Henderson after I'm gone. Our association won't do your reputation any good.''

''Do you think I care?''

''No.'' He laughed softly. ''But you should. In any case, I'm not sure how long I'll be around.'' He reached into the rear seat for his backpack. It didn't look very full.

He opened the car door. ''I'll find you if I have any free time before I leave.''

Olivia knew he was letting her down gently—he had no intention of looking her up. This was goodbye. ''But I still have your shirt.''

Her breath caught at the look in his eyes. His dark gaze drifted over her—and his flannel shirt. Then something in his eyes hardened and shut her out.

Drew didn't want the shirt.

The last thing he wanted was a tangible reminder of Olivia. He knew he'd never wear the shirt again without thinking of her.

"Keep it," he said.

When she opened her mouth to argue, he couldn't resist kissing her, one brief stolen kiss. The memory of her would linger, just as the sweet honey taste of her mouth lingered on his lips when he turned away.

A few moments later, Drew walked into the Trading Post.

Someone was coming out. Drew stood aside and held the door open to let the woman through. Her smile faded when she saw Drew. She lowered her eyes and brushed past him; her husband did the same. Drew had gone through twelve grades of school with both; now they pretended not to know him.

As others became aware of him, an awkward silence settled. Trying to ignore the reaction, Drew made his way down the narrow store aisle, gathering food and a few sundry items. Finally he set them down by the counter near the cash register. The clerk didn't look familiar.

"That it?" the teenager asked, after totaling the cost.

Drew nodded. He had a check from his younger sister that more than covered the amount. Abby had proved to be his only ally in the family. They'd never been close, and her loyalty had come as a surprise.

By now, a small knot of men had gathered.

One of them spoke. "So you're back. You fixing to stay?"

"Just passing through." Drew recognized the man.

"That's good." Reggie LaRoche was an independent logger. Over the years, he'd done a lot of business with the Pierces.

Drew said quietly, "I don't want any trouble."

Although middle-aged and balding, Reggie still looked fit. "That's a new one." The man never pulled his punches. "We don't want your kind around here."

Drew lifted an eyebrow. "My kind?"

"An ex-con," Reggie tossed back.

Drew caught his breath at the open show of hostility. He'd never been very good at turning the other cheek, but he gave it a try. "Look, I can't change what happened. But for what it's worth, I'm sorry."

Eyes narrowed, Reggie slid his hands into his pockets. "Well, maybe so, but don't expect anyone to roll out the red carpet."

Drew didn't have to be told.

At a nod from Reggie, the men stepped aside.

Feeling low and humiliated, unable to fight back in self-defense, Drew picked up the items he'd purchased and left.

Outside, the wind had picked up a nasty bite. It cut through his thin jacket, reminding him that he was in the north country, where autumn sped into winter.

With no means of transportation, he started the long walk home—a distance of five and a half miles from the heart of town.

A few cars passed before one slowed down, then stopped. It had a red light and a siren on the roof. The town sheriff got out. He nodded a greeting. "I heard you were back in town."

Eyes narrowed, Drew said coolly, "Word spreads fast."

Tall and erect in a uniform that proclaimed him the long arm of the law, Seth Powers tipped back his hat. "You know how it is. The Trading Post is still a hotbed of gossip. Anyway, it's good to see you again."

Drew's mouth tightened. "Don't give me that. In case you've forgotten, you arrested me and locked me up."

"I was only doing my job," Seth argued.

Drew laughed harshly. "Okay, fine, you did what you had to do. Now what? What do you want from me—absolution?"

"My conscience is clear." Seth drew in a breath, then started over. "Anyway, I'm glad you're home. You didn't let anyone know they were letting you out early."

"Three months short."

"That's good," Seth said mildly.

"The jail was overcrowded."

Seth laughed. "You haven't changed."

Drew met his gaze. "Yes, I have. I didn't have much choice. Wasn't that the whole point?"

"Yeah, I suppose. For what it's worth, I wish things could have been different." Seth wasn't long on sentiment—which was one of the things Drew had always admired about his old friend. "So now that you're here, how about a lift?"

Drew looked at the patrol car. "Unless I'm under arrest, I think I'll pass. The last time you took me for a ride, I wound up in the county jail."

"Just get in," Seth ordered in a low, deliberate voice.

Drew recognized the tone. He'd heard it often enough when they were on the same high-school football team. Typically Seth would crush any opponent, leaving Drew a wide open field to score. But this was no game.

"Sure, why not?" Drew said, accepting Seth's offer of a ride.

They drove off in silence. At the first—the one and only—intersection in town, Seth turned onto a secondary highway.

There wasn't any traffic.

After a few more moments, Seth said, "What are you going to do now?"

"I have no idea." Drew stared out the window, as if the answers were there. He tried to feel a sense of homecoming.

"You could stay," Seth said.

At the words, Drew denied the quick rush of emotion. There was no room for mushy sentimentality in his life—not anymore. He'd gone down that road before; it was a dead end. "No, I can't. There's nothing left for me here."

"There could be. After your family closed the sawmill, most people never recovered financially. With so many irons in the fire, maybe the Pierce financial empire can withstand that kind of loss, but it was the lifeblood of this town. While you're here, look around. A lot needs to be done."

Drew let Seth have his say, then responded, "I'm not the man to do it."

His mouth tightened when they passed the sawmill. Despite the warning, Drew was shocked by the hard evidence of decline. The main building was closed and boarded up. Heavy equipment stood rusting in the lumberyard. Once a thriving mill, it was only one of many owned and operated by Drew's family throughout the state. They'd simply shut this one down and walked away. They'd moved away rather than face the humiliation of their son in prison.

Now, taking in the locked gates, Drew suddenly understood the bitterness in Reggie LaRoche's eyes. No matter how far Drew went, he'd carry that expression with him, along with the knowledge that he'd helped put it there.

"It can't hurt to think about it," Seth said, then dropped the subject. After a moment or two, he cleared his throat. "Do you ever hear from Abby?"

The casual tone didn't fool Drew. "Occasionally." His younger sister had kept in touch, penning newsy little letters filled with anecdotes about her and her friends. As a result, Drew knew Abby better now than he had in all the years they'd lived under the same roof. But perhaps more revealing than her narrations were the things she didn't say. For instance, Abby never mentioned a boyfriend.

Seth kept his gaze on the road. "How's she doing?"

"You must have it real bad." Drew took no pleasure in the astute observation. Seth and Abby had dated. It felt like a lifetime ago; but apparently Seth still had feelings for her.

With an irritated sideways glance, Seth's face reddened. "She never forgave me for arresting you. What was I supposed to do? Resign?"

"She can be stubborn."

Seth released a sigh. "Tell me something I don't know."

In Drew's experience, there were always other women, but he didn't think Seth would appreciate hearing that. So he said nothing—neither did Seth.

Drew smiled slightly. Odd how they'd slipped so

easily into the old habit of nonverbal communication. They'd once been close friends, before events pitted them on opposite sides of the law.

During the trial, Seth had testified against Drew; so had Jared Carlisle and many others. Drew was found guilty of criminal negligence and safety-code violations. If he lived to be a hundred, he'd never live that down.

As he got closer to home, Drew felt his chest tighten at the sight of familiar landmarks. They passed Stone's End—the neighboring farm. It occupied the top of the hill, which always galled his father, Drew recalled now with a wry smile.

At one time, merging both farms had seemed like a good idea. Sam Pierce coveted all those rich timber rights, and Ira Carlisle was getting too old to run Stone's End. Marrying their children off made perfect sense—at least to them.

Drew had rebelled. He'd gone out of his way to annoy Ira's daughter. Jessie was sweet and gutsy and appealing. Drew had realized that a little too late. Then Ben Harding had come along. And the best man had won. Plain and simple.

"Ira passed away earlier this year," Seth said.

"I'm sorry to hear that." Despite their differences, Drew had always liked Ira Carlisle. Well, maybe "like" was putting it too strongly. He'd respected the man.

"He died peacefully. He married Dora Cummings a couple of years ago."

Drew shook his head in amazement. "Good old Ira."

When Oakridge came into view. Drew feasted his eyes on the sight. Along the road, sumacs flamed bright red. And in the distance, golden oaks vied with the sun.

"I'll walk the rest of the way," he said, aware of a need to be alone to savor this moment of homecoming.

"Sure." Seth pulled over, but kept the engine running. "The place is closed up," he warned.

"Thanks for the lift."

Before driving away, Seth said, "If you need anything else, give me a call."

With a nod, Drew watched the patrol car reverse. Then, taking a deep breath, he turned up the road. Within a few yards, a heavy steel gate with a No Trespassing sign barred his way.

Drew ignored it.

Half a mile farther, he passed an empty field where the migrant camp had once stood. After the explosion, very little remained—only the blackened shells of several small buildings.

Drew recalled a busy, noise-filled place, crowded with campers and tents and trailers, with children running about and laundry hanging out to dry, clotheslines strung up between trees.

And music.

There was always music.

At this time of the year, the farmworkers celebrated the end of harvest before they moved on. Secretly he'd envied them their freedom.

Now the silence was deafening.

Drew finally reached the house. It stood on a knoll, a handsome two-story house made of brick. Here again, the fire damage was never repaired. Half the house was boarded up.

He glared at the For Sale sign tacked to the front

door. Auction notices were posted on either side. He tore them down.

The lock seemed rusted; the key turned with a metallic protest. Once inside, Drew felt the chill dampness to his bones.

The house was empty, which he'd expected. His footsteps rang through the empty rooms, sounding hollow. He didn't belong here. He tried to feel something—anything. There was no welcome.

Memories of his childhood surrounded him. Right or wrong, they'd shaped him into the man he was today. In all honesty, Drew could think of no excuse for not turning out to be solid, dependable, generous—like his older brother. Evan was always first, always in charge. And Drew had rebelled, but that was no excuse. His father had come to expect the worst of his second-born son, and Drew managed to live down to his expectations. Boyhood pranks, fast cars and fast girls eventually led to careless business practices.

The explosion had been an accident—but one that might have been prevented with proper equipment maintenance. If only Drew had replaced that defective gas-tank valve, instead of repairing it, but he hadn't. He had to live with that knowledge.

Thank God, there'd been no fatal injuries. In his heart, he knew it was an accident. Had he paid enough, or would fate demand more? He'd destroyed Oakridge.

And his memories.

All the innocent days were gone.

After only a few hours in Henderson, Drew was determined to leave as soon as possible. However, he wouldn't get very far without his car, which a friend had stored for him.

He set out on foot for the neighboring farm. Hoping to avoid a run-in with any of the Carlisles, Drew didn't go up to the house. He soon located the abandoned barn Rachel had indicated in the letter she'd sent in care of his lawyer.

The red sports car gleamed in the drab interior.

Drew ran an affectionate hand along the fender, recalling the feel of the road and the powerful engine under his control. Had life ever been as simple as driving fast cars, flirting with pretty girls and long hot summer days that never seemed to end?

He checked the interior. The keys were under the floormat.

He was about to fit the key into the ignition when something moved near the open barn door. Alerted to the fact that he had unwanted company, Drew looked but couldn't see a thing. He felt a cold draft. He climbed out of the driver's seat, then closed the car door. The interior auto light went out, pitching the barn into blackness.

"Who's there?" he called out.

He suspected an animal seeking shelter from the cold, but he couldn't be sure.

Sweat broke out when he heard the cock of a shotgun.

Olivia could barely see more than six inches in front of her. Admittedly she was better with a handgun, but anyone could hit the broad side of a barn with a shotgun. She hoped.

Someone grabbed her from behind.

She felt a hard masculine strength. With a muscled

arm flexing around her throat, he dragged her against him. Knowing she had only seconds to strike back at her attacker, she elbowed him in the eye. His head jerked back at the impact. His hold loosened slightly, just enough to give her an advantage.

With one smooth move, she flipped him over her shoulder.

With a faster reflex, Drew hooked her ankle on his way down, and she landed hard on the dirt floor. He heard the rush of air from her lungs.

And her sputtering.

He felt like laughing.

Olivia.

What the hell was she doing here?

Before she could recover, he rolled her into the pile of hay, ignoring the sharp pricks and trying not to think of what breed of vermin occupied the shut-up barn. It smelled dank and musty, and probably hadn't been invaded in five years.

Like his heart.

"Olivia," he said, unable to disguise the surprise—or the pleasure—in his voice. He'd said good-bye to her so many times, and here she was again.

"Drew!" Her voice registered amazement; then she laughed, relaxing under his weight. A dimple played at the corner of her mouth. "Hello again."

He grunted. "I suppose you think this is funny."

She tried to sit up, but he was holding her down. She raised a hand to his eye. The tips of her fingers gently feathered his brow.

When he winced, she said, "Oh, I'm so sorry—I didn't mean to hurt you."

"You didn't hurt me," he returned, missing the

small connection when her hand fell away. "In case you haven't noticed, I won that round."

"I don't think so."

He heard the smile in her voice. Unable to resist, he dipped his head and kissed her, stealing her breath before she could catch it and talk back. Silencing Olivia took a lot of determination, but he was up to the task.

Long and slow and unhurried, he savored her sweetness. Kissing her could easily become habit-forming. He drew her close, fitting his body to hers with an ease that would have stopped him cold if he'd paused to think about it. He felt the slight curves, the dip of her waist.

When her arms crept around his neck, he knew he'd won this minor skirmish.

Chapter Six

The barn was cloaked in darkness. A draft came from the open door. Something scurried in the hay. Aware of a growing discomfort, yet drowning in pleasure, Olivia struggled to come back to her senses.

It was difficult when Drew was murmuring into her ear, sending a current down her spine, and easing his arms around her waist, pressing her closer. When his leg slid between hers, she almost came undone.

"Drew." Latching on to the last shred of self-denial, she placed her hands against his chest and found some breathing space. "What are you doing here?"

As if reluctant, Drew released her. His voice sounded husky, aroused and very male. "My car was stored in this barn. I came to get it." He dangled the key as proof.

Avoiding his questioning gaze, she glanced at the car. "But what is your car doing here?"

"Rachel is a friend…"

Her frown deepened. "Jared's wife?"

"Yes, but she wasn't his wife when I left Henderson. She was raising her sister's son on her own. I tried to give her the car outright, but she refused. Instead, she insisted on keeping it stored for me while I was away."

"That sounds logical, and just like Rachel. But how do you know her?"

"I've known Rachel for years. We met in our teens through her twin sister."

"I see." She sneezed violently. "What's that smell?" she said, when she recovered.

"Mothballs," he muttered.

She sneezed again. "What?"

He smiled ruefully. "I found some of my old clothes stored away in a trunk. I aired them to try to get the smell out."

Twitching her nose, she smiled. "You didn't succeed."

The sweater hugged the wide masculine set of his shoulders. The jeans were comfortably worn, not stiff, and fit snugly. He eased away, and she breathed a sigh of relief.

His gaze narrowed, as if it had suddenly dawned on him. "I explained what I'm doing here, now what about you?"

"It's a little complicated."

He drew in an impatient breath, then released it with a taut smile. "If you don't mind, I'd like a straight answer."

Olivia started to reply. "As I said, it's—"

At that exact moment, the barn door crashed open and drowned out the rest. A bright light blinded Drew when he looked around.

"All right," a deep-toned voice ordered. "Get away from her. Hands up, behind your head."

Then came another voice, a wizened, "Yep, don't try anything."

Recognizing both voices, Drew got to his feet and assisted Olivia. Together, they faced their audience of two.

Drew spoke first. "Looks like you got us."

Seth lowered his flashlight and exclaimed, "What are you doing here?"

"Don't ask," Drew said dryly. He felt like a kid with his hand caught in the cookie jar. "Fred, how have you been?" he asked the older man, a farmhand who was a fixture at Stone's End.

Fred said, "I can't complain. You don't look the worse for wear, considering...except for that eye." He set his hat back on his head. "Didn't know you were back home."

"As soon as I make a few arrangements, I'm leaving," Drew said firmly. How many times did he have to repeat it? He wasn't staying, and Henderson was no longer a place he called home.

"Well," Fred said, "you picked a mighty odd time of day to drop by uninvited. Looks like you came close to scaring the poor girl out of her wits."

At a glance, Drew decided Olivia didn't look scared or witless just embarrassed.

Her face grew redder as she explained, "I thought Drew was an intruder. I'm sorry. I called Fred before coming to check."

"And I called the sheriff." Fred frowned at Olivia. "I thought I told you to stay put."

"I was afraid whoever was breaking in would get away."

At that example of her logic, Fred shook his head. "Well, you got him, all right." Openly protective, he looked suspiciously from her to Drew. His gaze fastened on a piece of straw sticking out of her tangled hair. "Didn't know you two knew each other."

"We've met," Drew said, not feeling the need for further explanation.

Apparently Olivia did. She reddened several more degrees as she said. "I had some trouble with my car on the way home from Bangor. Drew was kind enough to assist."

"Odd. Seems to me it doesn't take two days to get from Bangor to Henderson."

Olivia hedged, "Yes, well. We ran into more car trouble. But everything worked out."

"Olivia was perfectly safe with me," Drew said in a dry voice. He folded his arms across his chest, then leaned back against the fender of the car.

Fred didn't look convinced. "Looks like we got here in the nick of time."

Seth chuckled. "I don't know about that. Looks like Drew got the worst of it."

Drew pressed a finger to his sore eye. He winced at the sharp pain. By morning, it would be colorful.

Olivia said, "I'm sorry." Her eyes were twinkling. "Would you like to come up to the house? The sooner you take care of that eye, the better."

"Come on, Fred," Seth said. "I'll drive you home."

After Seth and Fred left, Drew turned to Olivia.

Since meeting her, he'd gone from one absurd episode to the next.

He needed to get some answers. "You owe me an explanation. Before we were interrupted, you were going to tell me why you're here."

"Come up to the house. You need some ice for that eye."

"I'll survive a black eye," he said dryly. "Now can you please stop changing the subject? What's going on? And what are you doing at Stone's End?"

"I live here." She took a deep breath, "My father was Ira Carlisle."

"Try again." He shook his head.

"It's true. A few years ago, Jared found some old letters. With the help of a private investigator, they led him to me. Avis was my mother. Ira never knew about me. They were divorced before I was born."

"I see. And where does the DeAngelis part fit in?"

"When Mike married my mother, he adopted me." She smiled, as if recalling that magical day. "I became Olivia DeAngelis. I lived in a real house, with a fenced yard. Everything was great at first. But then my mother wanted to leave. I don't know how Mike did it, but he convinced her to let me stay. She said I could choose—so I chose Mike." She sighed. "I don't think she ever forgave me."

Faced with the irrefutable facts, Drew shook his head in amazement. "I've known the Carlisle family all my life. To my knowledge, no one ever mentioned the existence of a third child. Did you grow up knowing the family history?"

"My mother said my real father didn't want me."

"Hell!" Drew bit the one word out. And that was it.

Olivia laughed shakily. "No comment?"

"What can I say? You had a raw deal, and I'm sorry."

"I suppose they did the best they could."

He shook his head. "That's very generous of you."

"It's called self-preservation," she said with a rueful smile. "In any case, I'm glad you're here. Won't you come up to the house?"

"I don't think your family would be pleased to see me."

"They're all out of town. Besides, my family doesn't choose my friends."

Drew wanted to believe her. So why did he feel the need to push her away? Her identity had come as a shock—not a pleasant one. It made their relationship, however temporary, more complicated than he cared to examine too closely. And it was only bound to get worse if he saw her again.

"You said your adoptive father was a cop—didn't he ever warn you about getting mixed up with an ex-con?"

"No, he didn't." She smiled, her eyes clear and honest and filled to the brim with loving memories of the man who raised her and obviously gave her a strong sense of herself, as well as a generous, compassionate view of others. "As a matter of fact, he was a strong believer in rehabilitation."

"And what do you believe?"

She met his somber gaze. "I believe that most people deserve a second chance—all you have to do is take it."

Reminding himself that she'd fooled him once, Drew shrugged off her sweet concern. Like her innocence, it was tantalizing, seductive. After years of abstinence, any woman would have the same effect on him— No, he'd never felt this way before.

She wasn't any woman.

She was Olivia.

And she obviously needed protecting—from herself, from him and from her own generous heart.

There was one sure way to accomplish that.

"Look, before we go any further, you should know that I just got out of prison a few days ago."

"I know," she said, surprising him once more— although there *had* been that slight flicker of recognition in her eyes when they'd first exchanged introductions. But then, she'd covered it well, and he'd dismissed the suspicion.

"So you knew all the time?"

She nodded. "I haven't always lived in Henderson. But the explosion at the migrant camp is common knowledge. It was an accident, wasn't it?"

Drew blinked in confusion. "Yes, but I was charged and found responsible. Before we get to that, how about starting with the small fact that from the first moment we met, you knew my identity? You must have known where I spent the last five years."

"Well, yes...but I don't see why that should upset you."

"I'm not upset!" When she winced at the volume, he lowered his voice. "So why the pretense? Why avoid the issue?"

"I wasn't avoiding anything. You didn't seem anxious to rake up your past, so I was merely being polite." She looked sympathetic. "I can't imagine being locked up for any length of time. That must have been terrible.''

''I survived.''

''I don't suppose you want to talk about it.'' She clearly knew the details about his past, but she was asking him to open up and trust her. It was asking too much.

''No.'' His face hardened. His time in prison added up to five lost years he could never replace. He could accept it, make amends where he could and move on. Or let it destroy him. He couldn't share that fear with a living soul.

After refusing Olivia's offer, Drew went back to Oakridge. He planned to take care of some business in town and leave the following day.

He searched through the bedrooms and found a dry mattress, then dragged it downstairs into the den where there was a fireplace. Soon a fire blazed.

Once the house took on some warmth, he set about organizing the kitchen. Luckily the generator, which was kept in reserve for emergency use, still worked. His needs were simple, his grocery list basic—coffee, bread, cheese, apples. He'd fared a lot worse.

Later Drew stretched out on the mattress, unable to sleep, thinking of Olivia and her sad life. She was beautiful, with wide-set gray eyes and an effervescent smile.

She was also Ira Carlisle's daughter.

He assumed she'd inherited a share of Stone's End. Keeping the large produce farm operating efficiently, not to mention managing the rich timber resources, had to be a challenge. He wondered how she managed it with so little experience. Despite the evidence of family, she seemed curiously alone.

Drew knew the setup at Stone's End. He doubted much had changed while he was away. Olivia's brother, Jared, lived nearby, but he was away at the moment. He was a busy veterinarian, not a farmer. Drew recalled Ira resenting his son's lack of interest in Stone's End. On the other hand, her sister loved the farm—but Jessie had moved to Virginia when she married Ben Harding. Then there was Fred. And Ramon Morales was still around, managing the farm.

Five years earlier, Ramon had nearly lost his wife and child in the explosion at the migrant camp. Drew frowned at the reminder. Ramon would not be pleased to see him.

It was all so complicated!

Drew was sure of only one thing—he'd kissed Olivia, and she'd responded with every ounce of her delectable being. Drew tried to put that enticing image of Olivia out of his mind.

Gradually, with each deep breath, the day's tension faded.

He dreamed of her. After all the dark days, Olivia was a bright ray of sunshine, something he desperately needed.

But inevitably, after the daylight, night falls.

The following morning, Fred Cromie turned up early at Stone's End. He was not his normal cheerful self.

"Morning," he muttered, hooking his hat on a peg by the back door. Without waiting for an invitation, he pulled up a seat at the kitchen table and sat down.

"How about some breakfast?" Olivia offered.

"I sure could use a cup of coffee." He peered at her more closely. "You don't look too chipper."

Olivia reached for the pot of coffee. "I'm fine."

She poured a cup and set it in front of Fred. As her father's oldest, dearest friend, he'd assumed Ira's role as Olivia's protector, a situation Olivia accepted with grace.

Fred added cream and two sugars to the strong brew. He took a swallow. "So what's going on between you and Drew?"

Unsure, Olivia chose her words carefully. "He's trying to get his life together. I admire that."

"The point is…Drew Pierce isn't the kind of man you should be seeing."

"And what kind is that?" Olivia carefully set her cup on the saucer. "Hasn't he paid for one careless mistake?"

Fred shook his head. "Maybe he has and maybe he hasn't. Can't say I ever saw a skunk shed his stripes, have you?"

Despite her irritation at Fred's refusal to see Drew's positive qualities, she smiled. "No, I can't say that I have."

Fred didn't smile back. "You need to know that you're heading for a whole lot of heartache if you let Drew Pierce smooth-talk you into thinking he's changed."

Olivia guarded her natural instinct to spring to Drew's defense. "Please don't worry about me. Drew is no threat."

Before leaving town, Drew had to make a stop at the bank. He sat in the bank president's office and

stared at the contents of a safe-deposit box. He shook
his head in amazement.

Instead of the small trust he'd expected, he'd inherited blue-chip stocks from his great aunt, a
woman he hadn't seen in years.

"I never guessed she had so many," he said.
She'd never married and lived a simple life. For
some reason, she'd chosen him as her sole heir.

Wesley Tyler stared at Drew's black eye. "Have
you had some trouble in town?"

Reminded of his most recent run-in with Olivia,
about 110 pounds of trouble, Drew said dryly, "Just
a minor mishap. Now, about these stocks."

Wesley calculated the sum. The amount staggered
Drew. "She wanted you to have a fresh start."

A fresh start.

Drew absorbed the words. The money opened up
all sorts of new possibilities. "I saw the bank repos-
sessed the mill. What's the bottom price?"

"The farm and the sawmill are being sold as a
complete package." He mentioned a ballpark figure
that made Drew blink.

"What if I can raise it?"

"The auction is in three weeks. The place has been
on the market a long time. Getting it operating again
would take a lot of effort," Wesley warned, his lack
of approval obvious.

Drew smiled grimly. "Thanks for the advice."

He left the bank, then walked down Main Street,
aware of a stirring sense of familiarity. He stopped
outside the sawmill with its sprawling empty lum-
beryards.

The name *Pierce* was still emblazoned in gold on
the window of the main office building. Drew felt an

undeniable connection. He owed the town some restitution after the destruction he'd caused. And perhaps it all boiled down to a simple truth. If Drew didn't salvage the sawmill, who would? Who would put the town back on its feet?

He didn't have all the answers, but it wouldn't hurt to look around the sawmill, talk to a few people.

In an attempt to raise the money to buy the sawmill, Drew visited a car dealer, where he met with an unwelcome surprise. His car had depreciated in value. The proposed offer was a fraction of what he expected.

Like a lot of recent developments in his life, it wasn't what he wanted, but he'd settle for what he could get.

Several days later, Drew drove past Stone's End. Instead of continuing straight on the road toward Oakridge, he turned. At the abrupt maneuver, the car tires skidded on the loose gravel.

The old farmhouse stood on the hill like a silent sentinel, watching, judging him, as he turned into the drive. Apart from a fresh coat of white paint and a new front porch, the place hadn't changed much. It still felt like enemy territory.

Shaking off that thought, Drew climbed the porch steps, then knocked at the door.

Olivia greeted him with a surprised smile. "Drew, please come in." She was wearing a loose green smock, stained in a wide array of bright colors.

Drew stood there on the threshold, drinking his fill of her with his eyes. And with each delectable inch, he knew that he was only kidding himself. Although he wanted to buy the sawmill and atone for his mistakes, this was a good part of the reason he wanted to stay in Henderson. This sweet, exasperating slip of a woman.

"Hi, Olivia." With a crooked smile, he stopped resisting. He bent, intending to greet her with a casual peck on the cheek, but instead, his mouth homed in on hers. She'd obviously been sampling her own cooking. She tasted spicy. And hot.

Catching her breath, Olivia stood back.

"I was just finishing up for the day." Her cat curled around her ankle. She picked up the animal before it could escape through the open door, closing it firmly behind Drew.

"Nice cat."

"Jewel likes to roam. She's a house cat, but she doesn't seem to know it," she explained with a light laugh. She stared at his eye. "That looks painful."

"It looks a lot worse than it feels," he assured her. "I hope I didn't catch you at a bad time." His gaze fell on an untidy collection of fabric and dyes spread out on the table behind her.

"Not at all. Please excuse the mess." Olivia turned to the table. "It's easier to mix my own dyes than try to find the exact colors I need for each project. I was just finishing up for the day." She capped the bottles of dye, then stored everything else in boxes. "Give me a couple of minutes."

"I wanted to talk to you, but I can come back another time."

"No, this is fine. If you can stay, we can talk over supper." She removed her smock to reveal a red turtleneck and a denim skirt.

Drew slid his hands into his pockets. "Don't go to any trouble."

"I won't." She smiled. "Chili okay? It's been

slow-cooking all day. I'll only be a minute.'' She walked toward the pantry—a utilitarian section off the country-style kitchen. ''Make yourself at home.''

That was a tall order. Drew instinctively looked to the chair by the window. Ira was no longer there; yet the memory of his presence filled every corner of the room.

Chapter Seven

The house had been remodeled with gleaming hardwood floors, dotted with colorful rugs in warm earth tones.

Olivia's creations, Drew assumed.

She had several ongoing projects set up on wood frames. One rug in particular caught his eye. She'd reproduced a red sumac shrub in glowing detail, with shades of red ranging from reddish-orange to burgundy. He looked more closely, and found a red cardinal perched on a branch, blending into the leaves with striking simplicity.

Another nature scene depicted a dragonfly among the orange daylilies. A hummingbird folded its wings into a lilac bush, and so it went. Her artistic use of nature's camouflage was clever and subtle.

How much of Olivia lay hidden beneath the bright effervescent exterior? The question intrigued him.

Absently he picked up a sketch pad. He recognized the scene—a lake and a pair of deer.

When Olivia came back with a steaming bowl of chili and rice, she found him studying one of her sketches.

He turned to look at her, his gaze warm with admiration. "You never mentioned you were so talented."

Inviting him to sit down, she flushed with pleasure. "It's not finished yet."

Drew joined her at the round oak table. "And you sell these original designs?"

She nodded. "I have arrangements with several specialty shops on the West Coast. I also work with a couple of interior decorators. Those are guaranteed sales."

"You do all this by yourself?"

"I have an assistant, Rita Morales."

The name meant something to Drew—a reminder of all that had gone wrong. He didn't react outwardly, but warning bells went off in his head. What was he doing?

How could he think of a future when the past was still there to haunt him at every turn?

Apparently unaware of his tension, Olivia continued, "I've got great plans. I want to expand, add a workshop to the house. Some day, when I can invest in the business, I'd like to raise sheep and supply my own wool."

So she had dreams of expanding and turning her business into a larger enterprise—complete with raising her own sheep and spinning wool.

Spinning dreams.

Drew took one taste of the chili and choked. Olivia

handed him a glass of water. "I'm sorry, I forgot to warn you."

He drank the water in one long swallow before finding his voice again. "That's stuff is lethal. What's in it?"

"The usual. And a jar of hot banana peppers," she said with mock innocence. "And of course, I couldn't leave out some fresh jalapeño peppers."

"Of course." He swallowed more water.

She dropped a generous spoonful of sour cream into his bowl of chili. "This should cool it down. Maybe you'd prefer something else? I should have warned you I like it hot."

He smiled stoically and picked up his fork again. "This is fine. I'd forgotten food could taste this good."

"The recipe's Southwestern." She smiled back at him and picked up her fork. "My chili takes getting used to, I'm afraid. There's fresh corn bread," she offered. "And a tossed salad."

Drew helped himself to both before raising the subject of the farm. "I heard Jared was away. How do you manage this place on your own?"

"Ramon Morales has been managing the place for several years now. I don't know what I'd do without him. Then there's Fred, of course. Things are a little tight right now," she admitted, "but I'm sure next year will be better."

"Spoken like a true farmer."

"I'll take that as a compliment." The conversation dwindled out over dessert. "Coffee?" She handed him a cup, then stirred sugar into hers. "From what you said the other day, I thought you'd be gone by now."

"I was planning to leave, but something's come up that might mean a change of plans."

Her eyes clouded in confusion, softening the gray to shimmering pewter. "What do you mean?"

"I think I may have found a way to stay in Henderson. It involves reopening the sawmill. To do that, I need your help."

She shook her head. "I don't understand."

"It's fairly simple—a business deal."

Suddenly he couldn't continue under Ira Carlisle's roof. The old man's presence was everywhere. Drew's plan required putting aside old differences and entering into a partnership. He could clearly recall a time when his father and Ira had attempted to merge both families by uniting their children—Drew and Jessie—in marriage. And Drew had gone along with the plan. But that time had ended in dissension.

Now Ira's youngest daughter was in control.

While Olivia hesitated, Drew stole her next line.

"I have a business offer," he said, laying his cards on the table. "As you probably know, the sawmill is for sale."

Her eyes widened with apparent surprise. "It's been closed since I got here. Are you interested in reopening?"

"It's a possibility I'm looking into. But I can't do it alone," he said.

"But what does that have to do with me?"

"It would be simpler to show you. How about going for a walk? It's not that cold. And there's a moon."

Olivia looked up in surprise. "All right."

He waited while she put on a jacket.

"Where are we going?"

He grabbed her hand. "I want to show you something."

Outside, a full moon rode the clouds. Dry leaves crunched under their feet. The night felt cold, but not freezing. They didn't go far, just to the top of a knoll, where Drew stopped abruptly.

Placing his hands on her shoulders, he turned her toward a line of trees bordering fields. "There. What do you see?"

She frowned. "Is this a trick question?"

"No." He laughed. "You mentioned some plans to expand your business. That, Olivia, is the answer to your financial problems."

"I don't understand. It's only trees."

"Not just trees—ash, maple, oak and hemlock. Do you know what that timber is worth?"

She gasped when he mentioned a huge sum. "I had no idea."

"I want to reopen the sawmill. But I can't do it alone. We could do it together."

She turned to look at him. "But how?"

"We could be partners—business partners. If I can pull off the deal and buy the sawmill, I still can't raise the money to buy standing lumber up front. If you'd accept a bank note promising payment at the time of sale, we could both have what we want."

"I wish I could say yes, but it's complicated." She could see the disappointment in his face.

"Don't give me an answer right now. Sleep on it."

"That won't make any difference." Olivia didn't have the luxury of time to agonize over her decision. In one stroke, Drew had presented her with a problem and a solution. She could agree to his business proposal in exchange for his signature on a marriage certificate. The union would be temporary, just long enough to meet the terms of her father's will.

"I realize it's a lot to ask."

She shook her head. "It's not that. I'm sorry...I tried to explain last night." She clasped her hands together.

"There's no need for long explanations." His mouth in a tight line, he shoved his hands into his pockets. "Joining forces would mean taking a calculated risk on me. I don't blame you for being cautious. Forget I asked."

As he turned away, she grabbed his arm, wrapping her small hand around the bulk of his forearm, covered in a thick sheepskin-lined jacket. "Please don't be angry. It's not what you think."

Dark-haired, dark-eyed, he turned to look at her, his eyes wary. And suddenly her decision was easy.

"Let's not pretend," he said. "We both know I'm not a solid citizen with a spotless record. The thing is, no matter what happens, you'll get a sizable profit from the timber sale. That much is guaranteed."

She released his arm with an exasperated sigh. "It's not about the mill!"

"Let's not drag this out. You don't need to make excuses."

"I'm not making excuses. And this has nothing to do with your record, spotless or otherwise. It's not about you. It's about me. I'd like to help you, but you see, I don't own the deed to Stone's End."

He shifted impatiently. "Would you care to explain that?"

"Ira's will contains certain conditions I haven't been able to meet."

He raised a skeptical eyebrow. "Such as?"

"Marriage."

"As in love and marriage?"

She burst out, "You see how impossible it is."

He threw back his head and laughed. "Good old Ira."

She stiffened. "This isn't funny."

"Isn't it? What would you call it? Ira's still controlling fate. And there's not a damn thing you can do about it."

"Yes, there is." She buried her trembling hands in her pockets. "I don't have to break the will—I can meet the conditions. I can always get married. Then there would be no legal hang-ups or question of ownership."

Drew's eyes narrowed. "I didn't realize you were involved with anyone. Who's the lucky guy?"

She met his gaze. "You are."

He stared at her. "Are we actually talking marriage here?"

"Can you think of a better solution to both our problems?" Before he could say anything, she went on. "I suppose I could give up the farm, and you could give up any chance of reopening the sawmill, but what would that accomplish?"

"This is insane! Apart from everything else, your family would never approve. And with good reason. We're practically strangers."

"Of course, I care about Jared and Jessie. They've been very good to me, and I would never do anything to hurt either of them." Her voice revealed affection. "But I don't intend to live my life to suit them."

Drew noticed she didn't use the word love, even in regard to her brother and sister. From the bits and pieces she'd revealed about her early childhood, he could understand her need for security.

He tried to issue a warning. "Olivia, there are things you should know about me."

She lifted her chin. "I know enough, and nothing you say can change my mind. I know this is right. I feel it."

She felt it.

So did he.

He wanted to trust her. He wanted to believe.

"You will let Jared know about our plans beforehand?" he asked. That would give her brother an opportunity to raise any serious objections.

"If you think I should."

"Don't you?"

She frowned. "I suppose you're right. So does that mean you agree? Why should we both lose out when sharing my inheritance and combining forces would solve all our problems? This is the most practical solution."

Drew could see all sorts of problems rising out of their marriage, but he wanted the sawmill—and Olivia—badly enough to settle for a business arrangement. To acquire both he had to accept that a marriage of convenience was the only way to Olivia's heart. She was a Carlisle all right—ready to sacrifice all for Stone's End.

"It's a deal." Drew weighed his next words with as much objectivity as he could muster under these extreme conditions. "As long as you realize there are no rules against mixing business with pleasure." And to demonstrate exactly what he meant, he kissed her—long and slow and deep.

Olivia couldn't resist the gentle persuasion of his

mouth as he coaxed her lips apart, then explored within. All her plans had gone awry. But at the moment, all that mattered was this—this feeling of everything inside her rushing to meet him.

The following day, Drew stopped by the sheriff's office to inform Seth of his plans. "I've got some news."

Seth was poring over some paperwork on his desk. "I'm glad to see you're still in town." He leaned back in his chair. "I was afraid you'd leave without letting anyone know."

"I thought about it," Drew admitted. "But then I found a better reason for staying. I'm getting married."

The desk chair rocked when Seth sat up abruptly. "Run that one by me one more time?"

Drew folded his arms, then leaned against the corner of the desk. "You heard correctly. I'm going to marry Olivia. How about being my best man?"

Seth shook his head in apparent consternation. "Aren't you forgetting she's a Carlisle?"

At the reminder, Drew smiled tightly. "How could I?"

"You're not in love with the woman!"

"Why not?"

"Let's slow down a minute." Seth tossed his pen aside. "As I recall, you always swore to avoid the marriage trap. Now you're planning to marry someone you barely know. You've done some foolhardy things, but this makes no sense at all!"

"The reasons don't matter." Drew smiled. "Maybe I never found the right woman."

Openly skeptical, Seth shook his head. "So Oliv-

ia's the reason you've decided to stay in Henderson?''

Not prepared to spill his guts when he didn't fully
understand his own motives, Drew stood. ''There's
also the sawmill. I'd like to get the place operating
again. Most of the loggers are independents. Hopefully they'll come back. I've got a friend who's looking for a job.''

''Who's that?'' Seth asked.

''Some guy I met in prison.''

''Do you think that's smart?''

Drew shrugged. ''I owe Jack a favor.''

Seth shook his head. ''Well, since you're determined to go through with this, when's the big day?''

''Soon.''

Two weeks later Olivia stood on the courthouse
steps. She looked at her watch again. Anxious to get
past the formality of a marriage ceremony, she was
a few minutes early. For the first time, she worried,
what if Drew didn't show up?

Caught in a whirlwind, she hadn't told anyone of
her plans, not even Jared. She 'd decided to wait until
after the ceremony. He'd only attempt to stop her
from rushing into marriage with a stranger, a man
with a past. She couldn't bear to examine her motives
too closely. There would be plenty of time to deal
with those, as well as the inevitable inquisition, once
the merger was complete.

When Drew's dark green Blazer SUV pulled up at
the curb, she breathed a sigh of relief. He climbed
out of the car, then looked up and saw her. Unsmiling, he looked tall and formidable, and incredibly
handsome in a dark-gray suit.

His expression remained shuttered as he climbed the steps to join her.

She noted the new car. "I hardly recognized you without the sports car."

"I traded it in for something solid, not flashy." He smiled rakishly, thoroughly confusing her. "All part of the new image."

Was it only an image?

He handed her a corsage. "This is for you."

She couldn't look away, couldn't move, couldn't breathe. She tried to smile, but failed miserably. They'd agreed on no fuss. But here she was in her lacy shawl and white wool dress, and he'd brought her a delicate corsage of tiny red roses and baby's breath. At the sight of them, something in Olivia crumbled.

Drew threatened to breach her defenses. Instead of facing the frightening possibility that her heart was more involved with this man than she cared to admit, she buried her face in the flowers. She breathed in the sweet scent, restoring her courage.

This was no time for sentiment. She was close to getting exactly what she wanted, everything she deserved—Stone's End.

And nothing more.

While she absorbed that monumental realization, she managed a wobbly smile. "Thank you."

Drew stole her breath as he pinned the corsage to her dress. His knuckles grazed the rise of her breast, and her heart lost a beat, then started to race. At her helpless reaction, Drew met her gaze. Both looked away.

Drew took a deep breath and completed the task. "Ready?" He took her ice-cold hand.

She nodded. "If you are."

When they went inside, Seth was waiting. They exchanged stiff greetings. Aware of his disapproval of the proceedings, Olivia felt a growing sense of dismay.

A clerk looked up from her desk. "May I help you?"

"We have an appointment with the judge," Drew said.

"Oh, yes, a wedding. Do you have the license?"

So businesslike.

In a few minutes, they would exchange vows. It didn't have to mean anything, did it? As a child, Olivia had attended her mother's weddings—all of them. Avis had always claimed to be madly in love with the current man in her life. Someday her daughter would understand.

Well, Olivia was twenty-three and she still didn't comprehend how love could rob its victim of self-control, then self-destruct. But she knew it terrified her. Thank goodness, this marriage was only a legal formality. None of this was real. It didn't have to mean anything.

Like a litany, she repeated it over and over in her head.

The clerk ushered them into the judge's chambers. The room was large. Tall narrow windows let in the pale-gray light of a cloudy day. Artificial lights cast a harsh glare on the sparse furnishings.

Seated behind an official desk, the judge gave them an impersonal nod. "I understand you two want to get married."

Recognizing the man who presided over his trial,

Drew stood straighter. "Yes, sir." The judge had thrown the book at him.

This time Drew was prepared for a life sentence.

He wasn't sure if what he felt for Olivia could be termed love, but he knew she didn't love him back. Surely love couldn't exist under such adverse conditions. Olivia was prepared to sacrifice her freedom for Stone's End. And he was prepared to gamble on his future. How could he lose? He was acquiring the sawmill. A bride was an unexpected bonus.

The judge looked over the license. "I'm going to assume that everything's in order. That you've given this decision careful consideration."

"Yes." Drew's collar tightened a notch. He was wearing a charcoal-gray suit he'd found hanging in his closet at Oakridge. A thorough dry-cleaning had eliminated the odor of mothballs.

At Olivia's silence, the judge pinned her with a stern glance. "What about you, young lady? Have you thought this over?"

She cleared her throat. "I have."

"All right then." He got to his feet. "Let's get on with it."

Drew could feel Olivia trembling.

Under the circumstances, the rite of exchanging vows wasn't remotely romantic. And yet, each word bound them together.

The clerk served as a second witness. Drew repeated his vows firmly. Olivia murmured a shaky, "I do."

No one raised an objection.

With a few more words, they were married. "I now pronounce you husband and wife."

After it was over, Seth stood by, looking awkward. "Well, I should be going."

''Thanks,'' Drew said.

The two men shook hands. Seth kissed the bride.

Drew opted not to kiss his bride. Olivia looked so delicate and fragile. So tempting. But under the circumstances, kissing her might not be wise. This was about business. They had an arrangement, not a marriage. It was legally binding, with no room for emotional ties.

Drew placed his hand on her elbow and ushered her from the judge's private chambers. Moments later she stood outside. A blustery wind sent a chill through her.

''It's over,'' Olivia whispered.

Finally free of the soul-destroying resentment she'd felt since Ira's death, she felt curiously empty and at a loss to understand why. At the end of his life, Ira had given her a close-fisted share of Stone's End with a set of conditions that had driven her to find an extreme solution.

Ignoring caution, she'd married Drew, making it clear that he was merely a means to an end. But he was also her husband. Until this moment, she'd conveniently pushed that life-altering reality to the back of her mind, where Drew felt less threatening. How long would he be content to stay in that neat little compartment?

Chapter Eight

Once outside, Drew released his bride. His ego felt bruised and battered. Olivia had been completely honest; she'd married him for business reasons only. So why did he feel let down?

An edge crept into his voice. "All right. What's next?"

Her eyes widened at his tone, but she answered politely, "I made an appointment with my lawyer in Bangor."

"Right." He didn't really need a reminder.

With the auction deadline fast approaching, they had to stick to practical matters. They couldn't waste time in finalizing the legal conditions set in Ira's will.

She explained further, "We have an appointment with him first thing tomorrow morning. That was the only time he had free at such short notice."

"That doesn't give us much time to get there, unless we travel today.'' When she made no objection, Drew said, ''Then I'll make hotel reservations for an overnight stay.''

The day was relatively mild for fall; nevertheless, she shivered. Despite all the denial, he felt protective, possessive. He frowned at the crocheted white wool shawl she wore over her dress. ''Is that warm enough?''

She nodded, wrapping it closer. ''It's more practical than it looks.'' In her simple white wool dress and shawl, she was a tantalizing mix of sophistication and innocence—unconventional, but surprisingly bridelike.

''Olivia, are you okay with this?'' He searched her eyes for any sign of regret. ''Because if you're not, we can end this right now. It's only on paper.''

A paper marriage.

She stared back, her eyes a dark troubled gray. ''It's too late. We're married. Besides, it's the only way.''

A few scattered raindrops struck her face. They gleamed against her skin. She seemed shattered.

''Congratulations,'' he said. ''I know Stone's End means a lot to you.''

''You don't understand. You've always known who you are and where you came from. I never have. When I first came to Stone's End, I thought I'd found all that under one roof.''

''And did you?''

She answered indirectly. ''For the first time in my life, I knew why my eyes were gray, instead of pale blue like my mother's. Ira insisted that it would always be my home. Then, at the end, he added conditions.'' She clenched her hands into fists. ''Why should I give all of it up without a fight?''

Caving in at the evidence of her vulnerability, Drew took her hands in his, gently opening her fists until her palms rested against his. ''It's going to be okay.''

He knew his voice betrayed the same doubts she was obviously feeling. Had he made a terrible mistake?

Another one?

It was too late to turn back now.

After the ceremony, Drew went to Oakridge to pack a few things for the overnight trip.

Olivia went home to Stone's End. She'd already packed, but she wanted to change her clothes into something more casual for traveling. She climbed the porch steps, noting that the icy breath of an autumn frost had scorched the flower beds.

All the summer roses were gone.

She entered the silent house. For the first time in her life, she felt a sense of ownership. Stone's End was hers.

She slowly toured the rooms one by one, straightening a pillow here, a curtain there. In the front parlor, she found the family Bible. It held special meaning for her. As a bride, the first Olivia, her great-grandmother, had pressed a rose from her bouquet between the pages. Since then, each bride had followed suit.

Olivia removed the flowers from her lapel, then placed a red rose between the pages. She ran her hand lovingly over the gilted letters. Her eyes misted at the thought of all the Carlisle brides.

Perhaps she wasn't the most romantic or best-loved bride in the history of the family, but she'd done what she had to do in order to keep what was rightfully hers.

She turned at the sound of someone entering the house and calling out, "Olivia?"

"Hello, Fred. In here."

He entered the front parlor. "There you are."

Ramon Morales, who managed the farm, was with him. "Good day, Olivia," he said in his dignified way. "We got a better price on that last load of produce."

"That's good."

Fred said, "We just got back from the brokers. We stopped by to pick you up, but you'd gone out. Everything okay?"

"I had something important to do." Olivia took a bracing breath of air. "Actually I'm glad you're both here, because I have an important announcement to make."

Fred's gaze drifted to the Bible in her hand, then narrowed with open suspicion. "Well, spit it out."

"I got married." Olivia closed the Bible, trapping the rose between the thin, age-worn pages.

Half an hour later, when Drew arrived at Stone's End, Fred was there, along with Ramon. Both were seated around the oak claw-leg table in the kitchen. Neither was pleased to see Drew. The feeling was mutual.

A man of few words, Fred didn't beat around the bush. "Looks like you got a bargain. Proud of yourself, are you?"

Drew bit back a few choice words. The cockiness

of his youth had yielded to caution. "I'm not sure I know what you mean."

The older man bristled. "You saw a golden opportunity to get your hands on Stone's End. You took advantage of Olivia's soft heart!"

Drew's mouth went taut. "I'm sorry you feel that way. But that's not the way it happened." He knew better.

Beneath that fragile exterior, Olivia had nerves of steel and a brain that didn't allow much room for sentiment. He'd married her knowing all that, yet hoping her heart would make room for a husband eventually.

Olivia rushed to Drew's defense. "I've already explained everything."

Ramon Morales rose to leave. "I cared about your father. But I cannot work for Drew."

Faced with the man's obvious determination, Olivia said, "You'll still be working for me. I'm asking you to manage the farm. How about giving this some time?"

Ramon looked doubtful. "A trial period?"

She nodded. "If that's the way you want to look at it."

"What about him?" He nodded in Drew's direction.

"Drew's going to be too busy reopening the sawmill to get involved with the day-to-day management of the farm. I'll still need you, Ramon. You and your family have made a home here. I hope you will stay," she said with open sincerity.

Ramon sighed. "I will think about it."

She turned toward the older man. "And you, Fred. Stone's End wouldn't be the same without you."

Drew smiled grimly. So much for being partners. After getting everything she wanted, Olivia was dividing up the spoils.

Fred and Ramon regarded him with open hostility. Drew was suddenly afraid. He was going to lose Olivia. His hold over her was so fragile, so new. How could it survive all the censure and disapproval? They were bound to encounter more from her family.

To his surprise, Olivia moved to stand by his side. Perhaps she felt the same threat. Did that mean their marriage mattered to her? Or was this still about the farm? He understood her desperation, her need to feel connected to a place, a person.

He knew love had eluded Olivia all her life. She clearly felt threatened by strong emotions. And more than anyone, he knew the lengths to which she'd gone to keep Stone's End.

Acquiring a husband represented nothing more to her than the means to an end. How long would it take for her to regret their bargain?

"Drew and I are married," she said, surprising Drew with the firm tone. "I hope you can both accept that."

Ramon looked doubtful. Nevertheless, he said, "*Sí*, I will try."

Fred set his hat on his head. "Well, Ira must be rolling over in his grave. That's all I have to say!"

Drew felt Olivia stiffen under the harsh words. He placed a protective hand on her shoulder. "Now wait a minute!"

Small and slight, Olivia leaned against Drew. "Ira set up the conditions. He didn't leave me much choice. Lucky for me, Drew came along."

"No use arguing over spilt milk," Fred grumbled.

"This isn't getting us anywhere. We've got work to do. But just wait until Jared gets wind of this!"

On that note, both men marched out.

Olivia winced at the sound of the back door slamming.

She turned to encounter Drew's somber expression. Dealing with three irritated males was getting to be a trial of nerves. Despite the opposition, she was still convinced she'd made the right decision. Marrying Drew might be hasty, but it felt right, and she didn't care whether people approved or not.

Drew accused her softly, "You never told Jared."

Faced with his accusation, she swept her hair back from her brow. "I know. I just didn't have time to call him. Everything's been so rushed."

They both knew she was only making excuses.

She whispered, "Please don't be angry."

Drew released a long breath. "I'm not. Look, we knew this would happen. There's bound to be disapproval from all directions. Are you up to facing it?"

Olivia wasn't sure what problems he anticipated or why it should trouble him so deeply. "Yes, if you are."

"Then we'll get through it," Drew said, sounding confident. "All packed?"

"Yes, I just have to change. I won't be long." She was caught in a whirlwind, with no time to think—which was probably just as well. Logic might have brought sanity.

They drove to Bangor, where they checked into a Victorian inn. Drew had made the reservations. He'd never revealed a traditional side until now, which only emphasized how little Olivia actually knew about him.

Reminding herself that their relationship was strictly business, she tried to ignore the way the hotel clerk flirted openly with Drew. So much for remaining detached. This was no time to feel possessive. Hadn't she insisted on a practical, impersonal arrangement?

Drew handed her a key to her room. "You've got a room with a view of the river."

Her room.

"Lovely." She clutched the key. It felt cold and hard in her hand. They climbed the stairs to the second floor. Her room was three doors down on the left. His was the fourth. Was that a coincidence, or had Drew requested connecting rooms?

While she pondered that, Drew said, "Shall we meet for dinner? In the lobby around seven?"

"That sounds fine," Olivia agreed.

The room was a pleasant surprise. A charming arrangement of cherry antique furnishings, mixed with white wicker, gave it a timeless quality, a reminder of simpler, gentler times. In muted shades of lavender, blue and rose, the bed coverlet and canopy evoked images of elegant botanical gardens.

Olivia dropped her small suitcase, kicked off her shoes, then collapsed on the bed. She stared up at the flowered canopy, then closed her eyes. All she saw was Drew's face.

They were married. She should be pleased about that; but since her proposal, their relationship had changed. The magic was gone. Now there was uneasiness. He was polite—too polite. A cool detachment had replaced the warmth in his eyes. Drew probably thought she was mercenary, placing financial considerations above emotional ones. But when had her emotions ever served her well?

With a sigh, she rose. She was exhausted, yet too tense to relax. She'd feel better after a shower.

Unpacking her suitcase didn't take long. Since they only planned to stay a couple of days, she hadn't brought much—nightwear, something casual and, last, a special dress for dinner that evening. Suddenly she wished she'd packed something other than her favorite little black dress—"little" being the operative word. Too late now. Ignoring all the warning bells, she pulled the dress over her head.

The black silk made her feel feminine. And heaven knew, she needed every bit of confidence she could manufacture for the evening ahead!

At seven, Olivia went down to the lobby.

She didn't see Drew at first, then located him standing with his back to the room, staring out a tall window framed in velvet drapes. He looked tense. And alone.

Olivia paused.

She recognized loneliness.

Something deep inside her hurt at the realization that Drew had lost everything he held dear in life. Nearly everyone had turned against him, abandoning him to his fate.

Earlier today she'd witnessed the hostility he faced. He'd dealt with Fred and Ramon without a display of temper. He'd lost so much, yet she'd never heard him cast blame for his mistakes on anyone but himself. That took a certain courage and the will to make repairs. She wished she could help; she wished their relationship hadn't gotten so complicated.

As if he felt her presence, he turned and saw her. He didn't smile. His eyes slowly drifted over her dress, down the black silk stockings to her feet, clad in dressy black pumps.

By slow, aching degrees, her body came alive. The thin black silk of her dress felt heavy against her skin. Drawn by some intuitive force, too new and foreign to identify, she met his glance and couldn't look away. When a look of satisfaction lit his eyes, she took a deep breath and walked toward him.

She reached him and stopped, aware of an unexplained tension. Yet she didn't feel threatened. A tall window overlooked the city.

His eyes on her gleamed with masculine appreciation. "You look lovely."

Although the words were mild, his gaze made her flush. "I hope I haven't kept you waiting."

"I was just enjoying the view," he said, confusing her when he filled her in on some of the local history—until she realized they were playing a game of courtship.

"Did you know that three to four hundred years ago, millions of acres of virgin pine and spruce were logged out by a few big companies?"

She smiled. Although impersonal, the conversation made her even more aware of him. Noting the huge boulders and turbulent water of the river she could see through the window, she said, "The river doesn't look tame."

"It isn't. The rivers in Maine were used to drive cut logs down to the bay. They called it white-water logging."

Oddly captivated, Olivia turned away from the

window, toward Drew. "Where does your family fit into all this?"

"They came up the hard way. My great-grandfather worked as a camp foreman, while his wife cooked for the crew. Somehow, they managed to save enough money to open a sawmill in Henderson."

Absorbing his words, she realized the sawmill meant a great deal to him—perhaps as much as Stone's End meant to her. The knowledge made her feel connected to Drew. Strange how she could feel so drawn to someone she'd known for such a short time.

But perhaps time could be measured in terms of intensity rather than days or weeks.

Instead of voicing that new and very personal insight, she said, "So all this is in your blood."

He looked out the window, before turning back to her. "Yes, I guess it is. I never gave it much thought."

"Is that why you want to reopen the sawmill?"

"That, and the fact that *someone* needs to do it." As if she'd touched a raw nerve, he abruptly cut off the topic. "Shall we get a table?"

The dining room wasn't crowded. The atmosphere was Old World, elegant, unobtrusive. A string quartet played discreetly in the background. A waiter arrived almost immediately to take their orders.

Drew waited patiently while she made up her mind. After some consideration, Olivia set the menu aside. "I'll have the stuffed capon."

"And I'll have the prime rib."

"Yes, sir." The waiter took their menus.

Drew didn't need to look at the wine list. "And a bottle of champagne."

Once it was served, he poured two glasses, then handed her one. "I believe this calls for a celebration."

Olivia lifted her glass. "A toast."

With a taunting smile that could have meant anything, he raised his glass. A reflection of candlelight flickered in his dark eyes. "To us."

One sip of champagne made Olivia feel light-headed—or maybe that was her response to Drew's smile. Suddenly she wanted to know more about this man who had so captured her imagination—if not her heart. "Have you ever been in love?"

He set his glass down without tasting the contents. "Isn't it a little late for this sort of inquisition?"

"You don't need to answer. I'm just curious."

"Hasn't everyone been in love at least once or twice?" he said, not really answering her question. "How about you?"

"So far, I've managed to escape." She smiled, aware that she'd made love and romance sound like a communicable disease. Her mother's experience had immunized Olivia for life. She was surprised when he responded.

"All right," he said. "Let's get this over with. What do you want to know?"

Olivia shrugged, trying to sound casual. "I just wondered, what if you were to fall in love? How would that affect us?"

Only half-humorous, his smile concealed more than it revealed. "That's a nonissue."

Olivia hung on to her own smile. "Maybe not now. But what about tomorrow, next week? How do you know you won't meet someone? Hasn't there ever been anyone special?''

He leaned back, admitting, ''At eighteen, I fell head over heels for someone. I was sure I had all the answers.''

Her heart skipped a beat.

''What happened?'' Did she really want to know?

He shrugged. ''We split up.'' He made it sound so simple.

However, Olivia suspected there was more. ''You mentioned dating Rachel's twin sister. Was she the one?''

His mouth went taut. ''Yes, she was.''

Olivia stared down at her plate for a long moment before venturing further. She glanced up and found him watching her intently. ''Her name was Laurel?'' She had to know. ''And her son is Jared's son— Dylan.''

''Yes,'' he said, confirming the bare facts. ''Look, it's an old story. Laurel died many years ago. Rachel took over raising Dylan. Now, Rachel and Jared are married. I haven't heard from Rachel in years. End of story.''

Despite his cool detachment, Olivia suspected there was much more. She felt a surge of emotion. ''I'm so sorry.''

He looked surprised. ''Why should you be sorry?''

''Because you were eighteen and you loved her, and the whole affair must have hurt terribly.''

He released a breath. ''I was more furious than hurt.''

She lifted her glass to her lips. ''Mmm.''

Apparently unwilling to admit a weakness, he

glared at her for a long moment. Finally he laughed humorously. "All right, I was hurt. Satisfied?"

"Only if you got over her." She paused, holding her breath when she asked, "Did you?"

Drew searched his heart. "Yes," he admitted after a long moment. "Now are you satisfied?"

She smiled, her eyes soft and warm. "Yes."

Like a starved man, Drew absorbed that smile. It reached deep inside where no one had ever seen the pain associated with Laurel's betrayal. Olivia touched him as no one ever had. Her mention of Laurel had exposed a raw nerve, but it also forced him to examine the past and let it go.

The waiter served their meals. Over dinner, conversation drifted into less-sensitive areas, for which Drew was grateful.

But at length, he decided it was best to clear up a few more items. "I'm glad you mentioned Laurel. It points out that we are going to have problems convincing Jared and the rest of your family to accept this situation."

"Jared's entitled to an opinion, but I've been making my own decisions since I was seventeen. I don't need his approval."

Drew wanted to believe her. "While we're on the subject of family, are Rachel and Jared happy?"

"Yes, they're very much in love. They have four-year-old twin boys and a new baby girl. She's almost a year old."

"And Dylan?"

"He's terrific."

Drew smiled. "I'm glad. Rachel deserves to be happy. So does Dylan. He was always a good kid."

"Since you grew up together, you must know Jessie. She and Ben have a new baby girl, as well. Ira complained that he only had grandsons, so Rachel and Jessie each provided him with one granddaughter apiece. They were born within a few months of each other, less than a year before he died."

His smiled had disappeared. "And Ira was pleased?"

"Absolutely delighted. Everyone was."

Drew suspected her family wouldn't be nearly as enthusiastic about Olivia's choice of a groom, which worried him more than he cared to admit. Through thick and thin, the Carlisles stuck together.

Olivia might be a late addition to the family, but she'd already proved herself to be as single-minded as any family member when it came to preserving her heritage.

Chapter Nine

If Olivia had to make a choice between her loyalty to her husband or to her family, Drew wondered which she would choose.

The atmosphere in the dining room was romantic, ideal for a honeymoon. All the ingredients were there—a man and a woman. Champagne. A candlelit dinner. China, crystal and polished silver gleamed against damask tablecloths. All around, people conversed, laughed. Soft music played. It was discreet and low-key. It didn't intrude.

But suddenly Drew felt a million miles from Olivia.

She had his name on a marriage certificate.

What more did she need? What more did she want?

She'd given no hint of what she expected from this marriage, if one could call it that. Each time he touched her, he'd felt her response, but he'd made all the moves. So the question remained—what did Olivia want?

What would she give?

Would Drew be out in the cold in six months or less when she realized their marriage wasn't worth fighting all the disapproval they were bound to get? Did his getting a fresh start include Olivia? Or was this just a temporary fix?

Preferring to avoid that line of thought, Drew said, "We've discussed our families. Let's talk about us."

Her eyes widened. Self-consciously she pushed a lock of hair behind her ear to reveal a small gold hoop. She wore no other jewelry, he noted—except for the gold band on her left hand. All evening, he'd watched her twist it—as if it felt new and awkward on her finger.

"What about us?" she asked finally.

"We've got the legalities out of the way. That calls for some decisions, don't you think?"

At his determined tone, she sighed. "I don't see why things can't go on the way they are."

He raised an eyebrow. "Isn't that a little naive?"

She smiled. "How about practical?"

He chuckled, enjoying the banter. "How about dessert?"

She breathed a visible sigh of relief.

Drew knew she was just playing for time, trying to prolong the evening and delay a decision about which room they were going to use—his or hers, or both.

The waiter brought an array of desserts.

"What do you suggest?" she asked.

"The white-grape tarts with a zinfandel sauce are

a specialty of the house. The apricot-vanilla silk pie is also a favorite.'' There were more.

With the waiter's help, Olivia pondered over each one, then finally narrowed it down to a chocolate Victoria tart or a lily-of-the-valley white cake, so Drew ordered one and she ordered the other. ''We'll share,'' he said.

There it was again—that word.

Sharing.

Marriage was about splitting everything down the middle, then making it whole.

When dessert arrived, Olivia finished every bite, confusing Drew even more. If she wasn't delaying, what was she doing? Or was he reading too much into the situation? But one thing was clear—bed wasn't on her mind. Just his.

''Coffee?'' he offered.

She set her fork down. ''No, thanks. The meal was delicious.'' She politely thanked the waiter, Maurice. By now, they were on a first-name basis.

Vaguely amused by her apparent innate ability to collect admirers, Drew paid the check. ''Shall we go?''

In silence, they left the dining room, crossed the elegant lobby, then climbed the stairs. Their footsteps were muffled in the carpeted hall. Several decorative wall sconces made out of brass with tinted amber-colored shades lit their way.

Outside her room, Olivia turned.

''Well, here we are.'' Suddenly she felt awkward, as if on a first date. But she was married to this man. Would he settle for a good-night kiss and nothing more? ''Thank you for dinner.''

Instead of leaving it at that, he said, "Are you nervous about meeting with your lawyer tomorrow?"

"A little," she admitted, surprised that he'd brought up the topic. Until now, he'd shown little interest in her business arrangements. For some reason, she'd avoided the subject, as well. Perhaps she'd been attempting to put the reasons behind today out of her head. What would it be like to be a cherished bride? Well, she'd never know now.

"It shouldn't be that difficult to convince him we're deliriously happy newlyweds enjoying our honeymoon," he said with a touch of cynicism that didn't reassure Olivia at all.

Feeling anything but deliriously happy, Olivia leaned back against the door for support. Did it have to be all pretense?

He followed, leaning close, trapping her. His finger traced the thin strap of her dress, slipping it down over her shoulder.

He smiled gently. "If the honeymoon part has you worried, you have nothing to fear from me."

"I'm not worried," she said, her voice high.

He met her eyes. She wondered what he could read there, if anything. Her senses swam at his touch. Her heart raced when his hand traced the upper curve of her breast. His eyes darkened and she knew he could read every response. His voice dropped to a husky note. "Nothing's going to happen that you don't want. Do you understand, or do I have to spell it out?"

Her mouth went dry. "Yes, I understand."

Olivia knew he was going to kiss her; she could see the intent in his eyes. It began with a gentle caress, starting with his thumb smoothing the curve of

her cheek, tracing the high delicate bone that gave
her face its distinctive heart shape.

His thumb traced her lips, and she gasped. Feeling
deprived of air, she raised his mouth to meet his descending one. And the exploration continued until
she was clinging to him.

His hand drifted down her spine, drawing her
closer, letting her feel the power of his need; then he
released her. His eyes were like warm liquid pools
when they met hers.

He replaced the strap. No, he didn't have to spell
it out. He wanted her.

What did *she* want?

After Olivia parted from Drew, the question kept
her awake for hours. As a result, she overslept.

She had to rush to get dressed, which thankfully
left her little time to think about what Drew wanted
from her—apart from the sawmill.

Her blue wool suit was feminine but not fussy.
With it, she wore a white silk shirt. She fumbled
nervously with the row of small buttons, then added
a multicolored scarf. Olivia jumped when Drew
knocked on the connecting door.

Hurrying to open it, she nearly tripped on the carpet. Trying to appear calm and confident, she greeted
him. "I'm almost ready."

He checked his watch. "We don't have time for
breakfast. I ordered room service. Have you eaten?"

"No, but I'm not hungry." She couldn't possibly
think of food when Stone's End hung in the balance.
"I just want to get this appointment over with."

"It's just a formality."

"Yes," she whispered.

Then why the sudden attack of conscience? Why

did she feel guilty for using Drew? Her father had wanted her to find a husband. He'd left her no other choice.

They drove the short distance to the lawyer's office. It was raining. The entire northeast was caught in a huge bad-weather system. They'd decided to stay an extra day, hoping the storm would blow out to sea.

As they drove through the rain-washed streets, Drew said, "I've booked the rooms for a second night."

"That's good." Olivia was in no rush to get home, where so many problems awaited them.

It was much easier to pretend this was real—away from Stone's End. With no one to interfere, they were simply two people trying to get through the awkward early stages of a marriage—with only one minor complication. They lacked the most basic ingredient—love.

Nevertheless, the next few hours went smoothly.

With Drew in tow and proof of her marriage in hand, the appointment with the lawyer did indeed prove a mere formality. The marriage certificate, though crisp and new, confirmed that they were husband and wife.

Upon introduction, the lawyer shook hands with Drew, then smiled at Olivia. "So this is your young man. Looks like Ira was right, after all, and so was I." He chuckled. "I knew a pretty girl like you would have someone back home. I'm glad you took my advice and tied the knot. But I hope you haven't rushed into this just to settle the will."

Olivia was grateful for Drew's support when he took over.

He reached for her hand. "Once we decided to get married, there didn't seem much point to a delay. Isn't that right, honey?"

"Um, yes." For some ridiculous reason, Olivia blushed.

"Well, that's just fine." The lawyer indicated the legal papers on his desk. "We've gone over the terms of the will. Jared and Jessie have already signed. All it needs is your signature."

Olivia's hand shook as she added her name to the bottom of the will. She stared at the black script. She had everything she wanted. Almost.

There was only one awkward moment when the lawyer frowned at her signature. "Did you forget something?"

At a glance, Olivia realized she'd signed her maiden name. "Sorry about that." Red-faced, she corrected it.

She felt like a fraud—anything but a wife. Hand trembling, she dropped the pen, then stood back while Drew completed the legal form.

The lawyer added the date and his signature. "That's it, then." Apparently satisfied, he folded the marriage certificate, along with a copy of the will, into a long envelope, then handed it to Drew. "I hope you'll both be very happy."

"Thank you." Without examining the contents, Drew slipped the thick envelope into his breast pocket.

Olivia's lawyer added solemnly, "Maybe your father's methods seem unreasonable and unorthodox. But I know he was convinced it was the right thing for you."

On that somber note, Olivia and Drew drove back

to the inn. The temperature had dropped and the rain was turning to sleet.

Drew dropped her off at the main entrance. "There's no point in both of us getting soaked."

Disappointed when he failed to mention any plans to meet later, Olivia went to her room. She removed her suit jacket and hung it in the closet.

The time in the lawyer's office had been unsettling, bringing back memories Olivia preferred to leave buried. No amount of regret would change the course of her life. As a child, she'd had no control over events like her parents' divorce and all the confusion and lost years that followed.

When Ira died, she'd felt a deep sense of loss, wishing she could have had more time with him. There was never enough time. The terms of the will proved that he didn't trust her, a mere woman, to care for his precious Stone's End. How could Olivia believe in herself when her own father didn't believe she was capable?

She smiled ruefully. Of course, Ira was right, she didn't know anything about running a farm. She had to depend on others. Fortunately she had Jared and Fred and Ramon, as well as Ben and Jessie. She frowned. And now, Drew was added to the list. Could she depend on Drew not to let her down?

She simply didn't know.

She'd rushed into this marriage; she'd put her faith in Drew. Only time would tell if she was right or wrong.

Feeling chilled, she ran her hands up and down her arms. She ordered afternoon tea and sandwiches. The dessert menu tempted her to add a selection of tea cakes.

"For two," she tagged on, hoping that Drew would turn up.

A few moments later, when a knock came at the door, she threw open the door, but it was only the waiter.

She felt oddly let down.

After he left, Olivia took a seat at the small round table. She stared out at the sleet beading against her window.

The foul weather fit Drew's mood. After dropping Olivia off, then parking his car, he made a dash through the sleet for the front entry. Drenched within seconds, he swore when his foot landed in a puddle.

The lobby was nearly empty. His shoes squished on the stairs. Moments later, he entered his hotel room. His mood sank to a new low.

On a whim, he'd requested the bridal suite. Five years in prison must have addled his brain, he thought as he took in the fussy Victorian furniture, complete with white lace bedcovers and plump, heart-shaped pillows. It was the perfect setup for seduction. But he didn't have a hope in hell of bedding his bride. Drew stared out the window at the dismal weather.

He couldn't demand his rights.

Apart from Olivia's cool little act, a solid mahogany door stood between them. One turn of a brass key was all it would take. But who would make the first move?

When he shrugged out of his damp suitcoat, a long white envelope fell to the floor. He knew it contained the papers that legally bound him to Olivia. They'd cost him his freedom.

But what about the benefits—if any?

He bent and picked up the thick envelope. Weighing it in his hand, he glanced at the solid wood door. He crossed the room, lifted his hand and knocked.

In response, he heard a crash.

A small, hushed cry followed.

"Olivia?" When there was no immediate reply, he turned the brass doorknob. One twist was all it took. She'd left it unlocked. With a wry smile, Drew wondered if all of Olivia's objections were as paper-thin as their marriage.

When he entered her room, Olivia spun around.

"Are you all right?" he asked, reassured when he found her all in one piece.

"It's nothing. I just knocked over a teacup."

He took her hands in his. "Are you hurt?"

"No, I'm fine, really." When he ran his thumb along the back of her hand, she tugged it free. "I hope the china wasn't anything valuable."

"It doesn't matter," he said impatiently. "As long as you're okay?"

She nodded.

Suddenly he couldn't think of his reason for being in her room. Then he remembered. "Here, I thought you might want these." It was a lame excuse, but all he had. He handed her the envelope.

"Thank you." She slowly examined the contents.

"It's all there."

"I know." With a sigh, she set the papers aside.

He glanced at the table behind her—the two place settings. "Were you expecting someone?"

"Actually I was hoping you'd join me."

"I don't think that's a good idea." Drew edged back toward the door.

With a slight frown, Olivia followed. "Why not?"

With an impatient sound that sounded suspiciously like a groan, he said, "Olivia, do you know what you're inviting?"

Olivia tried to hide her disappointment.

She felt the unfamiliar but not unpleasant weight of a gold band on the third finger of her left hand. "We probably should have some ground rules. After all, we don't know each other very well."

"That's true." His eyes gleamed with cautious humor. "I have no idea where this conversation is going. But be warned, I have every intention of changing your mind someday."

She released a breathless "Is that fair?"

He smiled. "All's fair in love and war."

"Please, don't pretend."

"Who's pretending? In case you haven't noticed, this isn't a war—we've combined forces. I've been fighting the way I feel about you since the first moment you walked into that diner and picked me up."

She laughed shakily. "I did not!"

"I want this marriage to work. I think that means the whole nine yards, don't you?"

Promises. Promises.

Olivia's mother had never taught her daughter caution or patience. Olivia had learned those on her own...but perhaps she hadn't learned them as well as she thought because she was seriously thinking of making her marriage as real as it could be. She laughed, trying to hold on to one shred of sanity.

"Yes," she whispered, exposing her heart for the first time in her life to an overwhelming need to be one with this man who made her feel weak and strong at the same time.

Like a sorcerer, Drew had looked into her heart and found her weak spot. She'd longed for roots all her life. Could it be that Drew was the end of her long search?

Only time would tell.

Twisting the narrow gold band he'd placed on her finger the day before, she said ruefully, "I didn't expect to feel so…so married."

He nodded. The reality of their situation had obviously struck him, as well. He smiled with complete understanding. "Is that a bad thing?"

"Not exactly."

"Olivia, you still have a free choice."

She took a deep breath. "Well, then, in that case…" She walked toward him and straight into his arms, straight into his heart. How could he resist?

He didn't even try. He gathered her close. "There's something special going on between us. I've made some mistakes, Olivia, there's one thing I've learned, it's that life doesn't wait. I want to make love to you. You must know that. But this has to feel right for you. I don't want to rush you."

Her eyes clouded. "Isn't it a little late for that?"

"Perhaps, but this is new territory for both of us." He fingered the ends of the scarf around her neck. The swirling shades of blues and grays seemed to change the color of her eyes, like sunshine drifting over open water.

He slid the scarf from her throat.

Olivia swallowed hard. "On second thought, maybe you're right. We barely know each other. This is too fast."

"No, it's feels just right," he said, ignoring her

weak protest. "I've been waiting for you all my life."

The scarf drifted to the floor.

She watched it fall.

His voice betrayed a note of possession she'd never heard before, and it frightened her almost as much as it thrilled her.

He smiled when she remained silent. "Marriage can mean whatever two people want it to mean," he murmured. "We've observed all the conventions. We're married. Do you think waiting another day or a night is going to change the simple fact that I desperately want to take you to bed?"

She whispered, "I'm not sure."

"Trust me, it won't."

He dipped his head and kissed her, silencing her with a thorough exploration of her mouth, feeling a moment of triumph when she gasped.

Her hands crept up his chest, around his neck. She stood on tiptoe, reaching closer.

He pulled away for just a second. "If we're going to do this," he said, "let's get this part right."

Enjoying her bewildered reaction, he lifted her off her feet in one fell swoop and carried her over the threshold and into his room. Clearly the invention of a hopeless romantic, the high ceilings were bordered with garlands of flowers. She giggled helplessly at the cupids carved into the plaster ceiling, the heart-shaped wreath of dried flowers over the bed. With its lace hangings, the bed was an open invitation to seduction.

Drew said, "Don't laugh."

Olivia sobered abruptly. "I'm not laughing. I think it's lovely." Daring to touch him, she ran an exper-

imental hand over the hard lines of his face and
watched them soften. In wonder, her voice dropped
to a whisper. "But I don't understand. If you had no
intentions of making this marriage real, why the bridal suite?"

Ruddy color climbed his cheeks. "You know the
old Boy Scout motto—Be prepared."

"Were you ever a Boy Scout?"

He laughed. "No."

Chapter Ten

Olivia smiled, wrapping her arms around his neck and leaning close. "This is by far the nicest thing anyone's ever done for me. Thank you." And she meant every word. When their lips met, she put every ounce of persuasion into a kiss.

The flesh was weak—particularly a man's. Drew knew he was vulnerable. He was just going to have to take his chances and hope. Because he needed her.

He set her gently on the bed, following her down onto the mattress. "Don't look so terrified."

She caught her breath. "I'm not."

"Aren't you?" he taunted softly. "Marriage is a first for me, too. So stop looking like a frightened rabbit."

She laughed shakily. "Is that what I look like?"

His eyes roamed her heart-shaped face. "You look beautiful."

When his head dipped, she met him halfway. Like a delicate flower opening to the sun, her lips opened under his. He drank deeply, starved for the warmth of her. When he released her long enough to draw a breath, she ran a hand over his chest.

"Your shirt is damp," she whispered, reaching for the first button, then the second and the third.

She boldly slid her hand inside, running her fingers through the coarse hair on his chest. He shuddered at the gentle seduction.

Catching her hand, he stopped her. "Let's slow this down a bit." Drew wanted to take time to make love to her.

He physically ached with need.

But he wanted to savor every step along the sensual journey. Her shirt was tailored with long sleeves and a collar buttoned up to her slender throat. Drew turned her left wrist and unbuttoned the cuff, raising the exposed flesh to his lips. He heard her breath catch as he explored the delicate tracery of veins. Her right wrist received the same attention before he moved on to her throat. A row of small pearl buttons blocked his progress. A button lost its mooring.

And another.

His control nearly at the breaking point, he wanted to give her pleasure and delay the satisfaction for both of them as long as physically possible. But it was difficult when she was so responsive. He wanted to undress her and savor every delectable inch. The curve of her breast warmed to his touch; through the thin silk, the damp nipple puckered under his mouth. She gasped when his hands reached under the hem of her skirt.

Everywhere he touched, she responded. Long and

slow, the seduction went on. He removed her skirt, then the lace-edged camisole top, and felt her shock when cold air struck her naked breasts. The day was gray, but her skin glowed, all dewy pink and white. And finally, nothing lay between them.

They were both exposed.

He searched for words to make this right, but all he found was, "I want you."

In surrender, Olivia whispered back, "I want you, too."

His eyes grew tender. He kissed her mouth softly, barely touching his lips to hers. Only one mystery remained. A whisper of breath held her apart. He took her gently, aware that this was new for her. He felt her tension. It built, then exploded, all around him. And finally, he let go, taking his own pleasure. Bound together, they lay in a tangle of sheets.

Drew held her close to his heart. There were no words to describe how he felt.

In the morning, sunshine streamed through lace-dressed windows. Awake first, Drew ordered room service.

Hearing him on the phone, Olivia awoke. She stretched luxuriously—before she realized something was missing—her nightgown. She blushed rosily.

Drew laughed, leaning down for a kiss. "Morning."

"Um, hi." Olivia borrowed Drew's discarded white shirt.

Breakfast arrived.

"I'm starved," she murmured when the waiter was gone. She reached for a croissant.

With a lazy smile, Drew let his gaze drift over her. "Do you ever forget about food?"

She smiled. "Occasionally." Feminine and enticing in the masculine attire, she sat in a chair, her bare limbs exposed under the edge of his shirt. With her hair tumbled and her eyes still slumberous, she looked exquisite. He wondered what she was thinking. He knew every inch of her, but he had no idea.

"So what's the next step?" Drew had no intention of letting her evade the question. "We have a few minor details to discuss."

She spread raspberry jam on the flaky pastry. "I don't know what you mean." She took a bite. "This is delicious."

"For one thing, where are we going to live?"

"We?" Olivia responded weakly, not quite sure she'd heard him correctly. "Isn't that an awfully big step?"

"In case you've forgotten, we just shared a bed. Unless I'm wrong, the enjoyment was mutual. Or was it just sex for you?"

"Of course not, but that doesn't mean we have to actually live together."

A dab of raspberry jam lingered on her lips. He leaned forward and kissed her mouth. With the tip of his tongue, he removed the jam from the corner of her mouth. She gasped.

With a gleam of satisfaction, he released her. "My dear Olivia, I have no intention of setting this relationship back. We need to think about the future."

She nodded slowly. "All right."

"We are married, in every way. Apart from the personal side, we need to make a success of this business venture. If we don't present a united front, people will draw their own conclusions and know the marriage is a sham.''

Faced with a decision, Olivia set the remainder of her uneaten pastry aside. ''I assumed our living arrangements would remain the same. I don't see why our sleeping under different roofs should matter to anyone but us.''

''Ah, but it will. Henderson is a small town. As it is, I'll have trouble gaining back people's trust. It won't help if my marriage appears to be falling apart from day one.''

''I see.''

''Do you?'' he questioned. ''Let's not play games—after last night, we both know we're going to share the same space.''

Shaken by his intention to turn the honeymoon into a marriage, she said slowly, ''Then what do you suggest?''

''We could live at Oakridge.''

His suggestion shocked her. She'd never given any thought to moving out of Stone's End. How could he ask when he knew how much it meant to her?

''But part of the house was destroyed years ago,'' she said. ''And the fire damage was never repaired.''

He smiled. ''Right. Stone's End it is.''

How could she argue his logic?

They arrived at Stone's End in the late afternoon. The rain had finally stopped, and the sun was setting in a pink-tinged sky. An oak tree stood in front of the house. The limbs were stripped bare, autumn's last phase before winter. Yet miraculously trapped and dormant within all that bleakness lay the seeds of spring.

Drew dropped Olivia off. He had to go back to Oakridge. "I have to make a few arrangements, pack some of my things. I won't be long."

She reached across and kissed him. "I'll see you later."

It all felt so normal. She waved as he drove away. Once his car was out of sight, her hand fell.

Inside, the house felt cool. Olivia removed her jacket, grateful for the extra warmth of her cloudy-blue sweater, which matched her wool slacks. She'd only been gone a couple of days. It seemed longer. Her entire life had changed almost overnight.

Olivia ran her hand along the smooth marble top of the sideboard. The house was filled with furnishings. There were a few antiques, but none were truly valuable—except to her.

She went upstairs and unpacked, then prepared the spare bedroom for Drew. It had belonged to Jared at one time. Her only other choice was Ira's old bedroom. And somehow she couldn't put Drew there.

Jared's old room wasn't very large. The walls were painted warm ochre. The floor was polished oak, with a leaf-patterned hooked rug in shades of willow and brown by the bedside to provide some warmth and contrast. She placed fresh linens on the single bed, added an extra blanket for warmth, then fluffed up the pillows. Next she cleaned out the closet.

Her bedroom was just across the hall.

With a pensive frown, Olivia wondered if she was putting enough distance between her and Drew. Just because they were married and they'd made love once or twice—three times counting this morning's scene in the shower—didn't mean he could take control of every aspect of her life. Did it?

When Drew reached Oakridge, he saw an unfamiliar car parked in the driveway. He parked his Blazer beside it, then got out.

The front door opened.

His sister stood there. While their mother was small and fair-haired, Abby was tall and slender. She'd inherited her dark hair and pale skin from the Pierce side of the family. Her hazel eyes reflected her every mood.

Unsmiling, she spoke first when he didn't. "Hi. You don't seem very pleased to see me."

Drew smiled warily, unsure why she'd come. "I'm just surprised. How did you know I was here in Henderson?"

Abby slipped her hands into the slit pockets of her tailored wool slacks. "Actually Seth called me. I wanted to see you, so I came."

Drew climbed the porch steps. "It's been a long time."

She watched him with serious eyes. "Too long."

Drew corresponded with Abby in prison, but he hadn't seen her in five years. Drew was aware of her hesitation and wished it wasn't there. Abby was younger by eight years. When last seen, she was still awkward and shy, with the promise of beauty to come.

He didn't really know the woman standing before him. Another huge shock, another adjustment. "You've changed since I saw you last. You're all grown up."

She let out a small laugh, then choked on a sob and ran into his arms. "I missed you. I was so worried."

He held her. "God, Abby! Don't cry."

She buried her face against his chest. "I wanted to come and see you, but you refused to let me. Why?"

"I'm sorry." Drew hugged her tightly. He'd forgotten how emotional she could be—though she hid it well behind a reserved exterior. She was the only member of his family who had cared enough to stay in touch. "I didn't want you to see me in a place like that."

"Was it so awful?"

"It was no picnic," he said. "But I've put it behind me where it, belongs."

Wiping a tear from her cheek, she gave a wobbly smile. "That sounds wise."

"No one's ever accused me of that before," he said, hoping to ease the moment. "So how are Mom and Dad?"

Abby followed his cue. "Dad retired last summer. They're finally taking that cruise Mom was always talking about. It's sort of a second honeymoon."

"I'm glad." Drew meant it. His mother had raised a family of four. She deserved the leisure.

"Evan is managing everything while Dad's away."

"Naturally," Drew said wryly. His older brother was a model of perfection—honest, generous, hardworking. No matter how much he'd tried, Drew couldn't even resent Evan for it. "And what's Cal up to these days?"

"He finished college and joined the Peace Corps." She added a few details. "The last time I heard, he was in South America."

Drew chuckled. "Lucky Cal." The youngest of four, Cal had always managed to go his own way.

"Now, can you tell me what you're really doing here?"

Abby smiled ruefully. "Am I that transparent?"

"You may have changed on the outside, but I've never known you to act on impulse."

"I wanted to see you," she said, then admitted, "But I also needed to get away for a while. With a small casual shrug, she changed the subject. "Why did you stop answering my letters?"

"There was nothing to write about. You said Seth contacted you. Is he the reason you came home?"

Abby blushed. "Please don't read anything into it. I'm not sure he even likes me at this point."

"Trust me—he likes you." Drew's tone was dry.

"Seth said you were planning to get married."

Drew's eyes narrowed. "Ah, is that why he sent for you?" He took a deep breath, then slowly released it with the words, "Olivia and I got married two days ago."

His sister's eyes rounded in shocked disapproval. "When has a Carlisle ever brought good fortune to our family? Have you forgotten that Jared testified against you?"

"That's a separate issue. Olivia wasn't part of that period of my life," he said, aware that he wasn't being completely honest with himself. Any connection with the Carlisles had only brought him grief in one way or another.

Abby folded her arms crossly. "Exactly how long have you known her?"

"Long enough." Drew wanted Abby to accept his wife. "If you just give Olivia a chance, I think you'll like her. You might even find you have something in common."

Abby looked doubtful. "What's she like?"

The thought of his bride's complex and confusing personality brought a smile back to his lips. "She's artistic, practical, funny and sweet. And stubborn, just like all the Carlisles."

Abby shook her head in open dismay. "Oh, Drew. What on earth will people say?"

"It's bound to be a nine-day wonder until they find something more exciting to gossip about."

"If I remember this town correctly, that could take years," she said ruefully. "I've just got one question—are you happy?"

"Happy?" Drew tested the word on his tongue. It felt new and foreign. Freedom meant more than the absence of walls; it meant whatever a man dared to claim for his own, and that included a wife. Olivia was his. She just didn't know it yet.

Convincing her was going to be a real challenge, but he had a lifetime to work at it. Was he happy?

Drew laughed softly, realizing the unlikely truth for the first time. "Yeah, I guess I am."

That morning, Olivia had agreed that Drew should live at Stone's End, but she wasn't prepared for the reality of his occupancy. When he arrived, he dropped his luggage and a couple of boxes by the back door. One box was filled with books. Another with tools. A chain saw stuck out at an awkward angle, steel teeth gleaming in the dimming light.

Olivia switched on a lamp.

Trying for some form of normality, she said, "We haven't had a thing to eat since a late breakfast. You must be hungry."

"I'm starved. Do you need any help in the kitchen?"

"Can you peel a potato?"

He frowned. "I'm not sure."

With a firm, "I'll teach you how—it's easy," she handed him the necessary items and sat him down at the table.

Drew gripped a potato in one hand and the paring knife in the other. He wondered which end was up. In any case, it appeared he needed to learn a few domestic skills.

Olivia prepared a simple scalloped-potato-and-ham casserole. With it, she served tossed salad and fresh wheat rolls. Over the meal, the tension eased.

Drew mentioned that his sister had turned up unexpectedly. "I don't have any idea how long she plans to stay. She's renting a room in town."

Olivia toyed with her food. "I'd like to meet her. You should have invited her for supper."

"She had a date with Seth."

"The sheriff?" Olivia appeared highly intrigued. "Half the women in town have a crush on the man."

Drew dipped into his salad, forking a tomato wedge. "I hope you're not including yourself in that number."

Olivia said without hesitation, "He's not my type."

Under the circumstances, Drew didn't ask the obvious question. If he himself wasn't exactly her type, he didn't want to know.

"Abby's a few years younger than Seth, but she came home from her first year in college, and he flipped. They dated for a while," Drew said, leaving out the reasons for the breakup. "Seth's hoping to pick up their relationship exactly where they left off.''

''Do you think he has a chance?''

''I don't know. Abby was barely twenty back then. She's a grown woman now, with a strong will of her own.''

''I hope they work things out.'' Chin in hand, Olivia smiled. Openly inquisitive about his past, she leaned her elbow against the edge of the table. ''You never discussed your family. I'm interested, are there any more of you?''

''I have two brothers, one older and one younger. Simply put, Evan got there first. So I carved out a reputation of my own in town—the opposite of his.''

She teased him with ''Hmm, the local bad boy?''

''Right.'' His smile flashed. ''Then there's Cal. He's younger by several years, so he avoided the sibling rivalry. He's off in some South American jungle teaching the natives how to grow potatoes.''

''And your parents? What are they like?''

''They have a good marriage. Dad worked hard. His ambition extended to his three sons—which makes for some friction. My mother is the soft one, smoothing over the rough edges. She left a cushioned life in Boston to marry him. If she's ever regretted that decision, she's never wavered in her loyalty.''

''Are you close to them?''

He shrugged. ''They haven't forgiven me for messing up. Maybe someday. But first I have to prove a couple of things.''

''To them?''

''To myself. I've gotten a head start by getting married and settling down.''

''Do you think they'll approve?''

He shrugged. "Probably—once they get over the shock. The second step is getting the mill operating."

Olivia felt a sense of relief. The practical benefits connected to their marriage weren't all one-sided. Drew had as much to gain as she did.

They were finishing supper when the phone rang. Drew reached for it. "Hello." He recognized Jared's voice immediately.

As expected, Olivia's brother didn't sound too pleased at hearing Drew's voice. "So it's true. Bad news travels fast," Jared said. "I was hoping the gossips had it wrong."

"Does it have to be bad?"

Jared said harshly, "Could it be anything else?"

With no ready answer, Drew took a deep breath. "Olivia and I are married. Can't we bury the hatchet and try to get along for her sake?"

Jared shot back with a blistering "Not before I try and talk some sense into her."

Without another word, Drew handed the phone to Olivia. "It's Jared. Apparently he's heard the news."

She paled as she accepted the phone. "Hello, Jared."

For the next few minutes, she carried on a stilted conversation with her brother. Finally she said, "I know this must come as a surprise. The wedding was very small."

There was more as Olivia tried to explain the unexplainable. She'd married Drew in a matter of days after meeting him.

Drew looked across the table and met Olivia's troubled frown. She didn't look away. They'd made love. He'd felt the warmth of her touch, the seal of her lips, and knew there was more than a physical attraction between them.

After loving Olivia, there was no turning back. He could only hope she'd realize that what she felt was more than lust. Was she ready to accept their relationship? Did it go beyond contracts and bills of sale?

At length, she hung up.

"Jared and Rachel send their best wishes."

Drew shook his head in disbelief. "What else did he have to say?"

"He's teaching a class in wildlife at Cornell. He can't come home until the end of the semester."

Olivia got up and served dessert.

Neither said another word about Jared's phone call, but it was there between them—like a chasm that neither could breach. Conversation slipped into more general areas.

Olivia was good at keeping it light. Nevertheless, Drew felt her growing tension. After the meal, he helped with the dishes. Olivia put the food away, swept the floor, reset the table for breakfast, then asked if he wanted coffee and more dessert. Drew refused.

The cat curled up on Ira's chair and fell asleep.

Olivia hid a small yawn.

"Time for bed," Drew said, amused by her attempts to delay the inevitable. He'd persuaded her to share the same living space. He was under her roof.

The next move was up to Olivia.

"Of course." She glanced at his luggage piled by the door—as if seeing it for the first time. "Shall I show you to your room?"

Hiding a grin, Drew stifled the urge to toss her over his shoulder and carry her off to bed.

"Our room," he corrected her gently.

"Mmm." She backed away—toward the front hall and the stairs. When he followed empty-handed, she said, "Aren't you forgetting your luggage?"

"I don't need it tonight," he said.

True, she had yet to see any sign of pajamas in his wardrobe. She blushed at the reminder of his total lack of inhibition, while she still had a few shreds left. She'd discovered a surprisingly passionate side to her personality. Actually Drew had discovered it.

But was she ready to surrender completely?

"Don't you think we should slow things down a bit?" she asked. The back of her heel struck the first step. What had seemed so simple to Olivia only a few short hours ago now seemed terribly complicated. Sharing a bed occasionally was one thing. He was asking for more than that.

She could read the demand in his eyes when he taunted gently, "Slow things down—how?"

One by one, he backed her up the stairs.

They squeaked.

Chapter Eleven

At the top of the stairs, Olivia was out of breath. She waved him toward a door on the right.

"I aired out Jared's old room," she said without quite meeting his eyes. "I thought you might prefer some privacy."

The ball was clearly in her court.

The question was, was he prepared to let her get away with it? And was scoring points more important than ultimate victory?

Weighing his decision against the possible negative consequences, which he couldn't focus on at the moment, he said, "Where do you sleep?"

She caught her breath. "You said you wouldn't rush things."

He couldn't force her to share his bed. "Are we back to square one? I know Jared doesn't approve. Neither does Abby. If we're going to let everyone else decide how we live our lives, then this entire situation is pointless.''

She leaned back against the door. ''What do you mean?''

''I might as well go back to Oakridge, and we can be business partners and nothing more.''

''Why can't we compromise on this?''

''I've already compromised my life away.'' His mouth firmed. ''This is where it stops. You have to choose.''

She bravely met his hard gaze. ''Then I choose you.''

Drew searched her eyes for the truth and saw nothing but a clear, shining honesty. For now, she meant it. But he knew that outside opinion weighed heavily against him.

Their marriage was bound to be rocky because his reputation left a lot to be desired. In any case, she'd passed the first test. No doubt, there would be more; but Drew was determined to live in the moment. And that fraction of time was filled with Olivia.

Her bedroom was painted eggshell blue. Sheer ruffled curtains outlined the windows. And suddenly it seemed vital to make love on the big brass bed. The mattress was large, inviting. A colorful quilt lay at the foot.

Like an old memory, the scent of violets clung to it.

The following day dawned bright and clear. And cold. It was November now, a month of short days and long nights.

Unconsciously seeking Drew's presence in her

bed, Olivia rolled over and landed softly against a hard-muscled body.

For a moment, she lay there, absorbing the moment, the sense of belonging to someone. Surprisingly it didn't alarm her. Perhaps marriage wasn't so bad, after all.

She'd let Drew share her bed and so much more. In the end, her decision had been easy. She'd married Drew to keep Stone's End, but she'd discovered something special existed between them. She snuggled against him, feeling the angles and planes of his body cushioning her weight.

She opened her eyes to find him watching her. For some reason, she blushed, recalling the night they'd shared.

"Good morning." He smoothed the fine silk of her hair from her brow, tangling his fingers in the curls with apparent pleasure.

"Is it morning?" She smiled sleepily, wrapping her arm around his waist. "What time is it?"

"About seven. The auction starts in a few hours."

She'd forgotten all about the auction! But apparently Drew hadn't. For a moment she regretted their financial arrangement; then reality intruded.

But for their wedding bargain, Drew would be gone, out of her life without a backward glance. She tightened her arms around him. He responded by taking her mouth in a long, luxurious kiss.

He was classically handsome, with dark hair and sinfully irreverent dark-brown eyes. How could she resist?

She didn't even try. She sighed with pleasure when he bore her down against the pillows and enclosed her in a full embrace. Drew removed her nightgown, sliding his thigh between hers, pulling her close. Her skin felt hot wherever he touched. Her breasts felt tender, pressed against the crisp dark hairs on his chest. So many sensations...all leading to a pulsating moment of oneness.

Later, when Drew went downstairs, his good mood took a dive. Rita Morales was there. Apparently working on a project, with small strips of colored wool neatly piled around her, she was sitting at a table in Olivia's workroom.

Her back was turned to the door.

Drew hesitated in the doorway. He almost turned away. He knew that Rita worked with Olivia, but this was their first encounter since his return to Henderson.

He greeted her politely. "Good morning."

When she didn't respond, he tried again. "I'm sorry. I know I'm probably the last person you want to see. But I hope you can forgive me someday."

Only silence greeted his words.

Before Olivia spoke, he became conscious of her presence. She touched his arm. "Drew, she can't hear you."

"Why not?" He braced himself, but nothing could really have prepared him for what came next.

"Rita lost most of her hearing in the explosion. She's had surgery, but nothing helped. It's deteriorated since then."

His words echoed his heavy heart. "I did this to her."

"You didn't." Olivia's fingers tightened on his arm. "The explosion caused her hearing loss, not you." She moved toward the table and touched Rita's shoulder.

The woman turned around, greeting Olivia with a warm smile. Rita's expression changed, however, when she saw Drew. She was a small woman with dark hair and laugh lines around her mouth that crinkled when she smiled. She wasn't smiling as she looked at Drew.

"Tell her I'm sorry," Drew said harshly. "Hell, tell her I'd give my right arm if this hadn't happened to her!"

"She's deaf, not invisible. You can tell her yourself," Olivia said. "She can read lips and sign language. Just speak clearly in a normal voice. Stand close where she can see your face."

Drew approached. He looked into the woman's soft brown eyes and recalled her courage and her determination to save her son from the fire. "Can you forgive me?"

Without hesitation, she nodded. "I have my life. My son has his. God has been kind to us. It is best to forgive, and forget the past."

Stunned by her generosity, Drew explained, "I tried to apologize after the fire, but your husband was too angry to let me see you."

"*Sí*, Ramon is still angry. He couldn't protect us, and that still hurts him. I pray every day that he will find it in his heart to forgive the past."

"I'm sorry." With Olivia demonstrating, Drew signed the words. He circled his heart with a closed fist.

The auction started at ten in the morning.

The parking lot at the Grange Hall was nearly full

when Drew and Olivia arrived. Drew found an empty space.

They were late.

Nevertheless, Drew stopped Olivia from entering the large gray-stone building. "Be prepared for a little notoriety." His smile held a cynical edge.

Olivia could see the tension in his eyes. "I think I can manage that."

"I should warn you. It's the first time people will be seeing us together. They're bound to be curious. Think you can act like one-half of a happily married couple?"

Setting her misgivings aside, Olivia responded to Drew's direct challenge with one of her own. "I can if you can."

With a soft laugh, he dropped a kiss on her mouth. "You're on."

Olivia hid her concern. So much hinged on his being able to purchase the sawmill. If things didn't work out, would he leave town as he'd first intended?

A surprisingly large crowd had gathered at the Grange—a drafty high-ceilinged hall more typically used for social occasions.

At a glance, Drew recognized the owner of a logging company located in another part of the state.

Any competition meant a real possibility of failure.

A few independent loggers sat in a small cluster at the far end of the room, apparently aware that they had a lot at stake in today's outcome. So did Drew.

One of the loggers—Reggie LaRoche—looked around and saw Drew. With a disapproving frown, he nudged the man beside him. Whispers spread. Heads turned.

Ignoring them, Drew placed a protective hand on

Olivia's waist and nodded toward some empty seats in the rear of the room. His sister, Abby, was there—with Seth.

When Drew made the introductions, Abby was cool.

To his relief, Olivia pretended not to notice. "I'm pleased to meet you," she said. "Drew's told me all about you."

Abby's eyes flashed. "Funny, he hardly mentioned you."

At the direct hit, Olivia drew in a breath. "I know this all seems a bit rushed, but I hope we can be friends."

"I want my brother to be happy," Abby said, clearly not convinced his marriage could accomplish that.

"Believe it or not," Olivia said softly, "I want that, too."

Abby tightened her lips, but said nothing.

At that point, Seth put in a few words. "We heard about the auction and decided you could use some moral support."

"Thanks," Drew responded, grateful for his friend's attempt to ease the situation, and even more thankful for Olivia's tact.

In time, he hoped she and Abby could be friends. They didn't have a lot in common—except him. For the present, he deemed it wise to keep them apart.

With that in mind, he took the empty seat between the two.

The auction started with several bank-repossessed pieces of farm machinery. The backhoe went cheap. A parcel of land came up next. It sold fast. The

Pierce properties were among the last on the list, which meant they had to wait.

At noon, the sale was only at the midway point. Coffee and sandwiches were brought in. After lunch, the auction didn't resume immediately. Olivia took the opportunity to examine some of the china and cookware.

With Olivia occupied, Drew broke away to talk to some men clustered by the door. The auction had drawn a mixed crowd.

People were polite but distant, which suited Drew. Above all, he wanted to avoid a direct confrontation.

He braced himself when Reggie LaRoche greeted him with a curt nod. "I thought you weren't planning to stay in town."

Aware of Reggie's reputation as a ringleader, Drew shoved his hands into his pockets. With a shrug, he said, "I changed my mind."

That explanation clearly didn't satisfy Reggie. "Heard some tall tale that you and Ira's daughter got married. That can't be right, can it?"

"Actually the gossips got it right."

Reggie hid his surprise well. "Seems like an odd match."

Drew smiled. "Not to us."

Reggie took a moment to absorb that. "So what are you doing here? Come to watch the show?"

Drew saw no point in hiding his intentions. "I'm interested in buying the sawmill. If it works out, I'll need some loggers."

He let his glance drift over the other men, who had remained silent throughout the exchange. "I hope some of you will consider coming back to work."

Reggie said with some bitterness, "Your family left this town high and dry. It will take more than a few pretty words to get people to work for the Pierces again. Besides, I heard there's another bidder."

Drew shrugged. "I've got nothing to lose. I'm going to give it a shot."

"Good luck," Reggie said after a long moment.

"Thanks." Drew left it at that.

When left on her own, Olivia wandered around. She'd never attended an auction before.

Earlier she'd been surprised to discover it included an estate sale, some miscellaneous heavy equipment, as well as an impressive collection of antique glass.

One piece, a bluebird, caught her eye. When she reached for it, someone else did at the same moment. Olivia withdrew. With a small laugh, she said, "I'm sorry," and turned to find Drew's sister standing there.

Dressed in a gray wool pantsuit, her long hair simply clasped back, Abby looked casual yet sophisticated. Her clothes, hair, makeup, manicure—everything screamed class and privilege. Abby looked down, then held out the glass bluebird in her hand. "Were you interested in this?"

Feeling distinctly underdressed in blue jeans and a thick cardigan sweater, Olivia slid her hands into her pockets. "The crystal is beautiful, but you found it first."

Abby read the label attached. With a whimsical smile, she said, "It's the bluebird of happiness, guaranteed to bring the owner good fortune."

"What a lovely thought." When their eyes met, Olivia smiled back. "Perhaps we started out on the wrong foot. I know Drew cares about you. We need to get along for his sake.''

Abby's fingers curled around the bird. ''I suppose we should at least try.''

''This marriage must seem awfully rushed to you,'' Olivia said, trying to put the other woman at ease. ''I understand how you must feel.''

Abby shook her head. ''I don't think you do. How could you understand without knowing Drew any better than you do?''

''Then please explain him to me.''

''I love my brothers, all three of them.'' Abby carefully set the bluebird down among the other pieces of glass and crystal on the display table. ''I may be a few years younger, but I wasn't very old when I began to realize how hard things were for Drew. Everything came easy to Evan. When Drew graduated from college with a degree in forestry, he wanted to get into the family logging business, but guess who got there first?''

''Evan,'' Olivia said. She glanced across the room, smiling ruefully when Drew happened to look up. Did he know they were discussing him? She held his glance for a long moment, until he turned away.

Once released, Olivia took a deep breath. ''But they were just kids. Surely none of that has anything to do with the present.''

Abby insisted, ''Oh, but it does. Dad put Drew to work managing the farming side of the business— which Drew hated. So he messed up. And he paid a terrible price!''

''He's determined to put all that behind him. I'd like to help him any way I can.''

''You don't understand. I'm not making excuses

for Drew. He took risks and made mistakes. And people got hurt. Even in his personal life. But the mistakes weren't completely on his side. No one ever believed Drew was innocent of fathering Laurel's child.''

''Jared's son.'' It was a statement.

Abby nodded. ''I wasn't sure if you knew about Laurel.''

''Drew told me.''

Obviously surprised, Abby continued, ''He never talks about her. In any case, Laurel lied, and everyone believed her. It destroyed Drew's reputation, what was left of it. At some point, he simply stopped caring what people thought of him.''

Olivia smiled. ''He still doesn't.'' Oddly enough, it was one of the things she liked most about him. He followed his instincts. Perhaps his heart?

Abby interrupted that thought. ''All my life, I've watched Drew lose or settle for second best. He married you for reasons even he can't explain. Just once,'' she said passionately, ''I'd like to see him succeed.''

''I want that for Drew just as much as you do.'' Hoping to reassure Drew's sister, she added, ''I'm not going to do anything to hurt him.''

Abby's troubled eyes conveyed her lingering concern. ''I don't think you can help it.''

The auction resumed.

The collection of glassware soon came up. Olivia couldn't resist a pitcher and bowl. A few pieces of depression-era glass were added to her pile. Abby paid far too much for the crystal bluebird.

When the Pierce properties came on the block, the

bidding started low. A murmur rose when Drew made his first offer.

Someone quickly raised the stakes.

Back and forth it went, until the bidding came down to Drew and one competitor, the operator of the large logging company from another part of the state.

Seth leaned over. "Word's out they want to close the Pierces down and eliminate the competition."

With a silent nod to the auctioneer, Drew raised his bid. One more round, and he was out of funds. "That's as high as I can go."

Abby looked worried. "I have a little money."

"Thanks, but I can't take it."

"But I'd like to invest in the mill. I came prepared to stay and help wherever I'm needed."

"You'd hate it." Drew tried to let her down gently.

With a shake of her head, she protested. "I won't know that until I try."

Assuming she'd be bored in less than a week, he didn't argue. Abby wasn't exactly spoiled, but she was accustomed to a pampered existence. She'd never fit into the rough atmosphere at the sawmill. It would be like planting a cultivated tea rose among hardy geraniums.

"Going once!"

Olivia gripped his hand. "Drew, I have the farm. Why can't we use it as collateral?"

"No." He shook his head. "It's too big a gamble. There's no guarantee I can make this work."

"Going twice."

Leaning closer, Olivia set her chin. "I thought we were in this together. Partners."

His hand crushed hers. "You could lose Stone's End."

She paled at that, then firmed her resolve. "Only if the sawmill fails."

His eyes flashed a warning. "Don't you think this is carrying the act too far?"

Olivia suddenly knew it wasn't an act. Investing in the sawmill was one way of showing Drew she cared without putting it into actual words or risking a rejection. Emotional commitment wasn't part of their bargain. Drew was trying to recover a family legacy; so was she. They'd joined forces. Beyond that, there was nothing to keep them together.

She met his gaze. "There's nothing to discuss, really. We agreed to be partners. Besides, I believe in you. I know you'll succeed and make it work."

"You don't know any such thing," he protested. "Have you any idea what you stand to lose?"

Yes, she did.

She could lose Drew.

The admission shocked her.

Without the sawmill, Drew had no reason to stay. She wasn't enough to sway his decision. Without giving herself time to think about that, she raised her hand, upping the last bid. "It's a risk I'm willing to take."

She kept bidding until the one competitor dropped out. When it was over, she was co-owner of the sawmill. Olivia stood, flushed with triumph. "We did it!"

Abby wore a bemused smile when she handed Olivia the glass bluebird. "I got it for you. Think of it as a wedding present."

"Thank you." Aware of its meaning, Olivia held

the piece in the palm of her hand. The bluebird was exquisitely detailed. It was life-size, with wings outstretched and ready to fly.

Olivia looked up and met Drew's dark eyes.

He smiled wryly. "Would you like to see what you bought?"

Olivia felt like that small bird, frightened yet eager to face the next challenge.

The Pierce Sawmill overlooked Main Street.

Drew stopped and unlocked the gates before driving through.

Spread out over several acres, the lumberyard was the size of several football fields. When at maximum use, it was usually littered with timber in varying stages of processing, from freshly harvested to processed hardwood. Trucks and heavy equipment made up a good chunk of the Pierce inventory. Now they lay idle. Layers of rust had built up on some of the once-valuable pieces left exposed to the harsh elements.

There were several buildings—all closed up.

Drew parked in front of a weathered gray building. For a long moment, he stared at it, the enormity of the responsibility he'd taken on beginning to sink in. He felt inadequate, plagued by the memory of past failures.

For some reason he couldn't begin to fathom, Olivia had gambled everything on him. He wasn't sure how he felt about that.

He glanced at Olivia. "This is it."

She gave him a determined smile. "Let's take a look."

Olivia didn't want to miss anything.

Drew took her on a grand tour of the sawmill—well, maybe not so grand. Everywhere she looked, the old post-and-beam building showed signs of abandonment. Cobwebs clung to the ceilings, dust layered the floors and the chill November air blew in through several broken windows.

Olivia hid her growing dismay as she followed Drew from one area to the other. She'd invested in this?

No, she'd invested in Drew.

She'd done some impulsive things in her life, but this ranked among the top three or four. Marrying Drew was first.

Since meeting him, she'd done everything, short of hog-tying him, to keep him in her life. And like a fool, she hadn't stopped to figure out why—until she'd put Stone's End up as collateral.

More than anything, more than her legacy, Olivia wanted Drew. What should have been so simple was complicated beyond belief because she'd refused to see the obvious. Drew had come along at an opportune time, thus confusing the issue. He'd fit into her plans because he was the right man for her.

She'd used him.

Was it too late to undo the harm?

She desperately wanted a chance to make her marriage work.

They'd wound up in the main office. Olivia looked around absently. "Some paint would do wonders for this room."

"The place could use more than a little paint."

She laughed. "All right, a lot of paint."

When he didn't respond readily, she leaned against the window frame. "What's wrong?"

He turned to look at her. The light from the window behind him cast a shadow across his face. "My father occupied this office, then Evan. Those are big shoes to fill."

"I know you can do this."

He looked around the room. "Have you taken a good look? You just put up your precious farm for this place. It needs a hell of a lot more than a coat of fresh paint."

She folded her arms across her waist. "I thought it was what you wanted."

"I did want it. I was prepared to spend every last cent I had." He shoved his hands in his pockets. "But it was mine to lose! I didn't want your money."

His to lose.

Not hers.

Chapter Twelve

Olivia wanted them to build a life together. At first, she might have settled for the fringes, but now she wanted more.

Perhaps she should have put that in writing, she thought ruefully—which did nothing to solve the current problem. Drew didn't want her help.

Shocked by how much his rejection hurt, Olivia said, "But I wanted to help finance the sawmill. What's wrong with that?"

"Don't you get it?" He laughed at her confusion. "I'm not worth it! What if I mess this up?"

So *that* was it.

"You won't," she insisted. "I know how much this means to you. You'll make it work. I just know you will."

"Haven't you been listening? Everyone's tried to warn you. You could lose everything!"

Now she understood.

"But what if you succeed?" Olivia didn't know what else to say. Following her instincts, she walked toward him and watched him stiffen. "What if everyone else is wrong?"

"Hell!" With a hoarse laugh, he ran his hand through his hair.

"And what does it matter? We'd both be right back where we started? And we'd survive." She wrapped her arms around his waist and leaned close. "I believe you can do it. It's a risk I'm willing to take."

She was willing to take a risk on him.

With a short laugh, Drew clasped her tightly. "I must be going nuts, because you're beginning to make sense."

She smiled. "Don't sound so surprised."

"Okay, where do we start?"

To his amusement, she looked around. "Hmm, now about this room. I think pale-green, perhaps a celery shade, don't you agree? No, a soft buttery cream with all that dark wood."

Her enthusiasm was contagious.

With the beginnings of a smile, he said, "You're not going to let me wallow in self-pity, are you."

"Is that what you want?"

"No. Besides, there's no time to waste."

He looked around. "I have just one request."

"What's that?"

"No pastels. Remember this is a lumber company."

She smiled. "Then how about forest-green? I can put up some framed outdoor scenes to lighten it up."

She was awfully good at lightening things up.

She had years and years of practice.

Olivia found a rag and washed the filth from the glass on the front window overlooking Main Street. Gradually the letters, spelling out Pierce Sawmill, started to sparkle. She gave a final rub, then stood back to admire her handiwork.

Surprisingly, she felt a pride of ownership. The sawmill meant so much to Drew—she wanted to be part of it, part of his world. She hoped he'd let her be involved on some level.

Over the next few days, Drew placed ads in the Help Wanted section of several area papers. A couple of former sawmill operators turned up. Things began to take shape.

Getting the sawmill operating forced Drew to work long hours. To Olivia's discomfort, she missed him.

Armed with a paintbrush and a bucket of forest-green paint, Olivia arrived at the sawmill one day, prepared to redecorate Drew's office from top to bottom.

And just in case that wasn't enough to ensure her welcome, she brought an offering of food—fresh-baked muffins and a thermos of hot coffee.

"That looks wonderful," Abby said, taking a short break before returning to her self-assigned task of getting the antiquated computer up and running. She'd trimmed her nails and put her hair up in a clasp, but it didn't diminish her glossy appeal. "Did you actually make these?" She indicated the basket of banana-nut muffins.

"The recipe's simple," Olivia assured her with a warm smile. "I can give you a copy."

"Mmm." Abby laughed, admitting, "I'm not really into cooking. But these are delicious."

"Drew tells me you're planning to stay around for a while. I imagine Seth is pleased about that."

Abby's smile faded. "I'm not doing it for Seth. Does that sound selfish?"

"I don't understand. Why should it?"

Abby hesitated before confiding, "I don't want to give him any false hopes. I like Seth—a lot. But I'm not sure if I'm in love with him."

Although married, Olivia felt curiously inept when it came to matters of the heart. Nevertheless, she tried to sound reassuring and wiser than she felt. "Give yourself plenty of time. If it happens, it will feel right."

"Like you and Drew?" Abby returned with obvious skepticism.

"As strange as it may sound, the answer is yes. From the first moment we met, it felt right. I never had to explain myself to him. He just seemed to know." With the words, Olivia acknowledged what she'd known instinctively for some time.

"Does he feel the same?" Abby asked.

"I hope so." Olivia blushed, aware she'd revealed too much and unable to take back the admission. "Is he busy?"

"He's been closed up in his office since I got here."

Olivia grabbed a muffin, then filled a coffee mug. She walked into his office without knocking. Apparently annoyed at the interruption, Drew's brow wrinkled into a frown when he looked up from the pile of paperwork on his desk.

"Hi," she said cautiously. "How about a break?"

His irritated expression melted into a crooked smile. He tossed his pen aside, then leaned back in his chair. "Come to beard the lion in his den?"

She set the mug on his desk, then kissed him lightly—it was intended to be light. But at first contact, he groaned.

Taking her completely off guard, he pulled her down and kissed her long and thoroughly. His hand crept up from her waist, cupping her breast. He leaned farther back in his desk chair, rocking her against him. Where it all might have led Olivia had no idea, because the phone rang just when things were getting interesting.

Breathing raggedly, Drew dragged his mouth away, freeing her with obvious reluctance.

She stood up, straightening her blouse.

"Hello!" he barked into the phone.

Olivia felt extremely sorry for whoever was on the other end of the connection and pleased by Drew's response to her arrival. He obviously didn't mind her interrupting him at work.

Perhaps she hadn't needed the muffins, after all.

Drew finished his phone call.

By now Olivia had opened the can of forest-green paint she'd chosen for his office. The fumes blended with the odor of coffee and banana-nut muffins.

Drew rose and walked over to open a window. He breathed in, welcoming the fresh gust of cold air. Olivia could raise his temperature faster than any woman he'd ever known.

Moments later, when he went back to his desk, he watched her climb the stepladder, dripping paint in her glorious wake. Drew was aware of her—every living breathing inch—from the top of her golden head to the bottom of her dainty feet, plus every luscious curve in between.

"Come back here," he said, a wicked gleam in his eye.

Smiling to soften her refusal, she said, "We'll never get anything done."

"So what?"

She laughed. "Then you'll blame me. I came here to help, not to distract you from your work."

He grinned. "I'm already distracted. Now what?"

He stood abruptly, then came around the desk. She moved up another rung of the ladder, and he grabbed for her ankle.

Waving him off with her paintbrush, she laughed. "You wouldn't dare."

"Watch me." He toppled her into his arms. With a trembling laugh, she landed against his chest.

Caught between them, the paintbrush slid to the floor.

Her eyes were misty gray, filled with warmth and humor. Drew captured her mouth, silencing her laughing objections with a kiss that picked up where they'd left off only moments ago.

And the moments spun out while they explored the magic between them. It was still so new, so full of discovery—this tingling awareness, this need to be close—closer.

Reminded that this was neither the time nor the place to make love to his wife, Drew groaned when his sister's raised voice came from the outer office.

"I'm sorry, you can't go in there," Abby said firmly. "Drew is busy at the moment. Do you have an appointment?"

"I think he'll see me," came the amused response. It was a man clearly unimpressed with office protocol.

"And you are?"

"Jack Slade."

"I'm afraid your name isn't listed," Abby said. "If you'll wait here a minute, I'll check."

The humor disappeared. "Why don't I save us both some trouble and announce myself?"

"Mr. Pierce is a busy man. I'm not sure he has time to see anyone today."

Drew had heard enough. He needed to rescue his sister before she ran up against Jack's Irish temper. He released Olivia with reluctance.

Everything in their relationship felt so rushed, so crowded. For the first time in his life, he wanted to go slowly; he wanted to know what was on a woman's mind—besides him.

Olivia was maddeningly elusive, which he admitted could be part of the attraction. But it was much more than that.

She hid her insecurities behind a smile and a casual approach to life. Her childhood had been less than ideal. She bore the inner scars like a badge of honor, but none were allowed to show, and nothing got in her way when she wanted something. Beneath the warm generous exterior beat a passionate heart and a steely determination to succeed no matter what life threw at her.

She was a survivor.

So was he.

A few moments later, Drew found Abby, flushed and irritated, standing toe-to-toe with a tall, dark-haired man. To say that Jack Slade was a friend would have been exaggerating.

Jack didn't have friends. He was tough, with a hard, impenetrable shell. But he'd saved Drew's hide in prison when Drew came up against several inmates bent on bringing him down a peg or two.

"It's good to see you," Drew greeted the younger man, aware that he owed Jack a favor. He knew little about Jack's past, but he'd gleaned a few facts from the bits and pieces that had slipped out. Jack had grown up in a tough neighborhood and learned how to handle himself. Like a dog that's been kicked one too many times, he kept anyone from getting too close.

"I got your letter." Jack said, his blue eyes cold and deliberate. If anyone had ever loved Jack Slade, it certainly didn't show. "I could use a job."

Knowing Jack's circumstances, Drew sympathized. "What sort of work can you do?"

"Show me a motor and I can fix it. I've been working on a highway crew, driving heavy equipment. But that's done until next spring. I can drive a truck, and I'm willing to learn whatever will pay the bills."

Drew smiled. "I'm sure we can fix you up with something. Have you got a place to stay?"

Jack shrugged. "Not yet. I'll find something."

"There's a cottage on the edge of the lumberyard. It's empty if you want it."

"Sounds good. When do I start?"

"How about right now? I need all the help I can get. There's a ton of equipment needing repairs, not to mention this building. But first, I'd like you to meet my wife, and partner,'' Drew tagged on. ''This is Olivia.''

Her smile warm, Olivia approached Jack, her hand outstretched. ''Hi, Jack. Do you paint?''

He frowned. ''As in…'' His glance went from the paint down her front to a matching panorama on Drew.

Olivia flushed. ''As in painting walls.''

With a slow smile, Jack accepted her hand. ''I guess I can try.''

Drew inserted, ''And this is my sister, Abby.''

Abby didn't budge. ''How do you do?''

''Abby?'' Jack said just as coolly, ''Short for Abigail?''

She bristled. ''I prefer Abby.''

Having scored a point, Jack simply grinned.

Drew decided to intervene. ''The cottage is empty. You can move right in.''

Jack nodded. ''I'll get my stuff and see you later.''

After Jack left, Abby spun around and expressed her disapproval. ''How could you possibly want that man around?''

''Jack helped me when I needed it most. I'm simply returning the favor.''

''So you met him in prison. He's a criminal—he's obviously trouble!''

''He was innocent.'' Drew didn't know all the details, and he couldn't blame Abby for being concerned. Jack didn't have a visible ounce of softness and didn't trust a living soul. And who could blame him? He'd been framed for a crime he didn't commit, then freed when new evidence and a retrial found him completely innocent.

''Naturally. Doesn't every ex-con say the same

thing?'' Abby obviously realized what she'd said and gasped, ''Oh, God, I didn't mean you, Drew. I'm sorry.''

Drew took a deep breath. ''It's okay,'' he said, but it wasn't.

Abby's words raised all the doubts he'd tried to hide. The explosion had been an accident—but a direct result of his wrong actions—and he had to find some way to live with that knowledge. Prison had changed him. Each day had been a lesson in survival.

But Drew had discovered that some prisons were man-made and not made of stone. They were flesh and bone, with no way out, no escape from guilt and regret.

Now, for the first time in his life, he wanted to create order out of chaos. He wanted the sawmill to be a success. He wanted a home and stability. He wanted Olivia. Her investment in him put everything at risk. He couldn't afford to lose.

She'd put her faith in him, and that terrified him. What if he failed?

Sensing his pain, Olivia reached for his hand. Of course, she'd heard the entire exchange between brother and sister.

She felt helpless, caught in a web of old sorrows. Drew was obviously hurting. And all she could do was offer her support.

He had to heal himself.

On the way home, Drew turned onto a dirt road. ''I hope you're not in any hurry,'' he said to Olivia. When she didn't object, he stopped on an old abandoned logging road.

Olivia looked around. "I have no idea where I am."

"We're on Stone's End. I need to check out a few trees. We'll have to walk from here."

Side by side, they walked along the rough path, a steady rise. It was very peaceful. They walked to the top of the hill where the trees had been clear-cut and new ones planted. A brisk wind whipped up the dead leaves on the ground. The woods were alive. A mixed stand of oak, hemlock and maple covered an area of several acres.

Leaning back against a tree, Olivia caught her breath at the view, a valley with a river running through it. "This is truly beautiful."

Distracted, Drew smiled. "And it's all yours, Olivia." He dropped a kiss on her mouth. "Now let's get to work."

Olivia never met a tree she didn't like. A bemused Drew watched her stop and admire each tree, while he sized them up in dollars and cents—so much for each foot—according to scale. Most of the trees topped out at sixty to a hundred feet.

He stopped at a hemlock tree, using his eye to measure the girth and height. "This one should bring a good price."

She placed a protective hand on the rough trunk. "This one? Couldn't you leave this one standing?"

He tried to be diplomatic. "You see a tree. I see a house, books, paper or a piece of furniture that may become an heirloom. The trees will grow back. And Stone's End needs a steady income that isn't always at the mercy of Mother Nature."

"But it's such a tall, beautiful tree. How can you

think of cutting it down?'' Well insulated in down-filled clothing, her cheeks rosy from exposure, she looked lovely.

Sliding his hands into his pockets, Drew tried to keep his mind on business. ''Which ones do you suggest I cut down? The ugly ones? The short ones?''

''Wouldn't that be more logical?''

''Not if you want a decent return on your investment.'' Aware that Olivia was facing the reality of her decision, he smiled to soften the blow. ''May I remind you that we are not clear-cutting? We're replanting and leaving small to midsize trees with more room to grow.''

''And that cuts down the risk of forest fires. I know all that.'' Silently she looked up at the tree, then winced when he spray-painted a red mark at the base, and another several feet higher.

Drew felt like the bad guy in a B movie. ''Olivia, I'm sorry. It has to be this way.''

''I know,'' she said in a small voice, suddenly aware that he could be single-minded and even ruthless where his business was concerned. It was a side of Drew she'd never seen before. She wasn't sure she liked it. She'd examine that later, but right now he obviously expected a little more enthusiasm from her.

With a forced smile, she brushed her misgivings away, at least for the moment. ''So how does this work? I mean, where do you fit into the operation?''

At her cooperation, his smile looked relieved. ''For now, I'll be doing a little bit of everything. Fall is a good time for logging. The leaves are down. The ground is hard.''

"What will you do when the weather turns colder?"

"Dress warm," he said, with a flash of his quicksilver smile, "and pray for an early spring."

Suddenly spring seemed awfully far away to Olivia. How could she possibly plan that far ahead when each day seemed like a tightrope balancing act?

Over the next few weeks, the logging operation got underway. Once work began, Olivia saw even less of Drew. Up before daybreak, he rarely got home before midnight, long after she was sound asleep.

While Fred and Ramon managed the day-to-day operation of the farm, Olivia worked to catch up with her holiday orders. When she stopped to think about her marriage—which was often—it seemed that their relationship was in a holding pattern, giving them a much-needed breather from the intense emotions that had driven their relationship from the start. It all made perfect sense.

Unfortunately Olivia wasn't thinking with her head. With or without Drew's presence, her heart was constantly under siege by new emotions she'd never acknowledged before, and her defenses were crumbling.

One day, the old house shook to its very foundations as a large truck carrying a load of cut timber rumbled past the front door. Suddenly, she needed to see Drew.

She stared out the window to the distant treeline where she knew he was working that day. She'd missed seeing him that morning. She missed him now.

Giving in to the impulse, she dressed in warm

clothes, layering jeans and a thick wool sweater with a down vest. She laced on a pair of workboots.

An inch of fresh snow covered the ground when Olivia set out from the house. The air was crisp and cool; the scent of pine woods tickled her nose. She hiked uphill into the woods along an old logging road. The surrounding brush had recently been cleared and the track widened for use. Signs of activity were everywhere.

The deep silence of the forest was split by the shrill discordant sounds of a chainsaw mixed with the mechanical drone of a skidder hauling trees.

Approximately half a mile from the worksite, she passed the landing where the logs were cut to length. From there, they were loaded onto a truck for delivery to the sawmill. At a distance, Jack was operating the skidder, hauling logs to the landing.

Jack waved both arms when he saw her.

Olivia smiled and waved back.

She never heard him shout, never saw him jump down from the skidder and run after her.

Chapter Thirteen

The deafening buzz of a chain saw grew closer. Olivia climbed over a rotting log, then ducked under a low branch. Suddenly she lost her direction. She spun around, but every tree looked exactly like the next one. It took her a long moment to realize the chain saw had cut out. All sound had died.

An intense hush suddenly filled the air around her.

She heard a faint sigh—hers?

A soft rustle of undergrowth broke the lengthening silence. Twigs snapped, then came a crack, a huge groan. It seemed to come out of the ground. The wind sucked past her.

Olivia turned, horrified to discover it wasn't the wind at all, but a large oak tree on a downward spiral, its bare limbs outlined against the brittle blue sky.

Everything around her trembled as limbs tore from

nearby trees. Nothing slowed the tree's descent. An inaudible cry escaped her. She heard shouts. They filled her ears, along with an inner roar.

"Run!"

Terror struck.

She stood, frozen.

Jack's frantic shouts alerted Drew.

Not breaking his running stride, Jack pointed to some bushes. "Drew, to your left!"

Drew spun around. He could barely see the top of a golden head. God! Olivia had appeared out of nowhere. She stood squarely in the path of the falling tree.

His heart stopped, then beat like a drum in his chest. He dropped the chain saw, then raced toward her, pouring everything he felt into one terrified shout. "Olivia!"

The hoarse sound tore from his throat.

Through the roar in her ears, Olivia couldn't hear Drew, but she watched his face contort with anguish. He was racing toward her.

With a muted cry, she reached her arms out to him just as he reached for her. Lifting her off the ground, he ran for safety.

With limbs outstretched, the tree followed, its length easily outpacing their puny efforts to escape its furious descent.

Suddenly Olivia was falling, and Drew was covering her with his body, sheltering her from the crushing weight. If they were lucky, they might escape the main trunk.

The ground shuddered as the tree came to a resting place. With the earth cold and hard at her back, Olivia found herself trapped beneath Drew.

She freed one hand, relieved to feel a pulse in his throat. "Drew, Drew!" she said frantically, her voice barely above a whisper. "Are you all right?"

At her touch, he opened his eyes. "I... God, are you okay?"

More concerned with Drew, she released a shocked breath of relief at his return to consciousness. "I think so."

"Good. Olivia, I..." He started to say something else, then stopped. Apparently overcome by pain, he closed his eyes.

"Drew!" When he made no response, Olivia's voice rose with alarm. "Drew, can you hear me?"

Jack came running up. "You okay?"

"I think so." She stared at him, feeling helpless and terribly frightened. "But Drew isn't."

"Did the tree hit him on the head?"

"I'm not sure. It all happened so fast! It's all my fault. If only I hadn't—"

Before she could get any further, Jack said, snapping Olivia out of her misery, "There'll be plenty of time for that later. First things first. Right now we just have to worry about getting you both out of this mess."

He quickly sized up the situation, then cleared away the branches and limbs trapping Olivia and Drew beneath them.

Olivia didn't know Jack Slade very well, but forced to rely on him, she was glad he was there. "What do you want me to do?"

At her submissive tone, he actually smiled, reassuring her with the words, "I'll get you out in a minute. Just don't move. I'm going to check Drew first. There could be some broken bones. Or a head injury.''

After checking and finding no evidence of a serious injury, he carefully lifted Drew. ''Looks like you both got lucky. The main trunk missed you both by inches.''

Lucky?

Like one of those hapless, star-crossed lovers in an old forties' screen gem, Olivia didn't feel very lucky. In fact, good fortune seemed to elude her. Drew was hurt. Somehow he'd become the center of her world. Losing him was unthinkable. With his weight removed, she was able to breathe more freely.

Nevertheless, her voice shook. ''Please be careful,'' she said. ''He's obviously hurt.''

''What about you?''

With Jack's help, she scrambled to her feet. Brushing off his concern, she felt shaken, but insisted, ''I'm fine.''

A moment later, leaning over Drew, she unzipped his jacket, then unbuttoned his shirt. She slid her hand inside, relieved to feel a strong heartbeat against the palm of her hand.

Jack shook his head. ''Looks as though he got off easy with just a few cuts and bruises.''

''Then why is he still unconscious?''

''He probably just passed out.''

Olivia frowned in amazement. ''He fainted?''

''From shock,'' Jack defended his friend. ''He probably has a dislocated shoulder. That hurts like hell.''

With Jack's reassurance, Olivia felt only slightly better. ''Well, we still need to get him to the doctor. He needs to be checked.'' Jack tried to lift him.

At the movement, Drew moaned and opened his eyes. All he saw was Olivia surrounded by sky.

With a soothing hand, Olivia bent over him and brushed his hair from his brow. "It's okay, love, I'm here."

Love?

Drew's head was spinning. Had he died and gone to heaven?

Jack cracked a grin. "A few inches closer, and that would have been it. You saved Olivia's life. You're a hero."

That brought Drew back to earth.

The terror had receded, but he glared at Olivia. Her face was pale. "Don't ever do that again!" he rasped, blinking in agony. Something inside was hurting. Some internal organ—more than likely his heart. Why, he wasn't exactly sure, but it had something to do with Olivia. "Do you hear me?"

God, she was going to be the death of him! But he'd never felt so alive. He hauled her down against him and kissed her senseless. By the time he released her, the adrenaline rush had worn off. Drew became conscious of a sharp pain tearing through his shoulder. He welcomed it; it kept him from facing his feelings. He'd come so close to losing Olivia.

The next few hours were a blur.

Cradling his arm close to his chest, Drew insisted he could walk out of the woods. Jack went ahead to get the car, then came back to pick them up.

At the house, Olivia fashioned a makeshift sling, which eased the pain. "Drew, you should have an X ray. The closest hospital is in Stillwater."

"I'll drive," Jack volunteered.

Thus, with Drew in the passenger seat and Olivia

curiously silent in the back seat, Jack drove the distance. He assured Drew that there was nothing to worry about—business would go on as usual—which only made Drew worry more. He'd managed to hire back some millworkers and a supervisor, but there was no set routine at the sawmill. Jack had little experience at cutting and hauling wood, and Abby still hadn't figured out how to update the old computer files, much less add the new ones.

They were all doing their best.

Olivia had called ahead to the doctor, who was also an old family friend. Dr. Peterson was waiting at the hospital in Stillwater when they arrived. After checking Drew over, he ordered some immediate tests.

A nurse wheeled Drew away.

The doctor, an elderly man with a gruff voice and a no-nonsense manner that hid a soft heart, turned to Olivia. "Now what about you?"

"There's nothing wrong with me." Her gaze followed Drew until he was out of sight.

"That's good to hear. And don't go worrying your head about that young man of yours. He's going to be just fine. Looks like he wrenched his shoulder. Probably did a job on a couple of tendons while he was at it," Dr. Peterson said. "Drew never does anything halfway."

"He will be okay?"

"We'll fix him up." He looked at her chart where the admitting nurse had jotted a few items after taking Olivia's vital signs. "Now it says here that your pulse and temperature are normal. Blood pressure looks good.'' He glanced up under bushy eyebrows. ''Anything hurt?''

Accustomed to his curtness, Olivia smiled. ''No.''

He penned something on her chart. ''I heard you got married. Surprised I didn't get an invitation.''

Olivia apologized, ''We kept it small.''

''Well, Drew was never one to stand on ceremony.'' He shook his head. ''Young people are impatient these days. I suppose love can't wait.''

''Well, there were some practical considerations.''

Dr. Peterson narrowed his eyes. ''You know, I brought that boy into this world. He was born premature, five weeks early, as a matter-of-fact.'' The doctor chuckled. ''He's been in a hurry and trying to catch up ever since. Sometimes that blinds him to what's right in front of him—until he gets hit over the head with it.'' He shook his head. ''Practical, my eye!''

Olivia smiled. ''I can't imagine him as a little boy.''

''Well, I can tell you one thing—he nearly drove his mother nuts, what with getting into one scrape or another. He was small for his age, and kind of puny. Always trying to keep up with the bigger kids. Then he sort of grew into himself.'' The doctor chuckled. ''Still accident-prone, though. Reckon he's still growing. Takes some people longer than others.''

With a bemused smile, Olivia absorbed that, while the doctor walked off. After a moment or two, a nurse came back and told Olivia she could go home. However, Drew had to stay.

Olivia went back to the waiting room.

Jack was thumbing absently through a magazine.

He stood when he looked up and saw her there. "Well, what's the verdict?"

"His shoulder injury is serious enough to need emergency surgery. It's nothing major, but he can't go home until tomorrow." She frowned, admitting her concern. "He's going to be furious—probably at me for causing all this trouble."

Jack stared at her for a long moment. Just when she thought he wasn't going to comment, he said, "He's damned lucky to have you. If he doesn't know it yet, then he's an idiot."

Jack's endorsement came as a complete surprise to Olivia. Although gratified, she couldn't help but wonder who was the idiot. She'd fallen in love with her own husband—and didn't know how to tell him!

When Drew learned he needed surgery, requiring at least one overnight stay, he wasn't pleased. Fortunately the anesthesia provided a few hours of welcome oblivion.

By the following afternoon, he'd recovered enough to know he wanted to go home.

The hospital room had "institution" written all over it, reminding him of his time spent locked away in prison. The walls were green, the bed was metal, and Drew had been issued a number. It was tagged to his wrist.

His twenty-four hours were up, and he wanted out.

Olivia was late.

A perky brunette in a white uniform and squeaky shoes arrived to take his blood pressure.

Chafing at the delay, he wasn't surprised when she raised an eyebrow and said, "Let's try that again."

Drew took a calming breath. "Okay."

"Much better."

Then Olivia walked in, and Drew's pulse went up. The nurse smiled. "Never mind. You'll live."

At the comment, Olivia looked worried. "Is anything wrong?"

"That's my line. You're late."

"Five minutes!" She said out of breath. "I drove right past the first time. I'm not that familiar with the area."

Somewhat mollified by her explanation, he said, "Now that you're here, can we leave?"

The nurse objected, "But we haven't discharged you."

Drew grabbed his jacket. His left arm was in a sling and temporarily out of commission.

"I'm discharging myself." And he walked out.

Left behind, Olivia glanced at the nurse. "Is there anything I should know about any further treatment?"

"The doctor left instructions for hot and cold packs, a light diet and a prescription for pain medication." The nurse handed over a sheet of paper with the list.

"Thank you." Clutching it in her hand, Olivia caught up with Drew by the elevator.

"Are you sure you're all right?"

He turned his head to look at her. "Don't I look it?"

Restraining the urge to touch him, she smiled. "Actually you look as if you got hit by a freight train."

"Or a tree." He pulled her against his side, then turned his head to stare into her eyes. "It could have been worse."

He kissed her temple. His breath stirred the fine gold tendrils of her hair. He didn't say another word.

He didn't have to.

Olivia knew exactly what he was thinking. They were both lucky to be alive—and together.

By the time they got to Stone's End, Drew was clearly in pain. He tossed back a couple of painkillers with a glass of water. He refused Olivia's offer of assistance with the removal of his sheepskin-lined denim jacket and shrugged out of it after a minor struggle.

Feeling helpless, Olivia stood back and watched him. "Is there anything else you need?"

He tossed the jacket on a chair. "I'll be fine after I catch up on some sleep."

"You're sure?"

"Olivia." His tone was mildly exasperated. "Please don't fuss."

"All right." She clasped her hands behind her back.

Drew watched her lovely face close up and regretted his curt dismissal, but he simply couldn't handle Olivia, the physical pain radiating down his arm, and his feelings all at the same time.

In the bedroom, he stretched out on the bed.

The room was filled with sunlight. He stared up at the shadows on the ceiling. Sounds of Olivia moving around below drifted up the stairs. She turned on some music and hummed along. Her voice was soft, soothing.

He closed his eyes. His chest rose and fell. For the first time since the accident, he could breathe freely.

He was shocked to admit how good it felt to be home. And Olivia was at the heart of it.

Was it all temporary?

He didn't have the answer, but one thing he knew. Like everything else he'd once valued in life, it could all disappear in a heartbeat.

Later Olivia found Drew flat on his back in their bed, sound asleep and fully clothed. Apparently he'd been unable to remove his shirt and jeans. He hadn't asked for any help.

For some reason, that hurt. She didn't have much experience caring for someone. For most of her life, she'd been too busy struggling to survive under less-than-ideal conditions. She tried to suppress the memories of missed school events, the late meals, the forgotten birthdays, the unpaid rent, all the times she'd expected her mother to be there, all the times she wasn't. Those were Olivia's earliest memories.

They'd shaped her past. And at times when she felt most vulnerable, they haunted her still. As a result, she'd never let people get too close. But Drew had breached all her defenses. He'd made her care.

She'd lost so many people in her life. What if she lost Drew?

Until the accident, she hadn't understood the dangerous aspects of his line of work. Despite the mechanical aids, it was still primitive—man against nature.

One error, one slip, could cripple or end a life. Her carelessness had almost cost Drew's life. But he was safe now, and so was she. Or was she? He'd risked his own safety for her, which posed an all new risk.

What if losing Drew hurt more than loving him?

Right now, he was here in her bed, in her life.

After breaking down her resistance, he didn't want her wifely concern. So what did he want? A partner? A lover?

What if she wanted more?

The small crystal bluebird sat atop her dresser, gleaming under a night-light. Happiness eluded her. With a wistful smile, Olivia settled into her rocking chair to watch Drew sleep.

A frown marred his brow; and she worried, was he in pain, despite the prescribed pills? Did he ever dream of her? She leaned her head back and closed her eyes. So this was what it felt like to love someone, to wonder and worry and dream. To share his pain. Of course, she loved Drew.

The realization brought her no comfort.

The room grew cooler.

The chair rocked…and squeaked. At the sound, Drew stirred restlessly.

"Come to bed," he whispered into the silence.

"I thought you were asleep," she whispered back. Why the hushed tones when they were both awake escaped her at the moment.

She climbed into bed, careful not to disturb him.

"I was asleep, but I woke up." He used his good arm to draw her closer. "I just want to hold you."

She tucked her head into his shoulder, her hand crept under his shirt—she needed to feel him. "You could have been killed."

Drew felt her nearness to his bones. "But I wasn't." He wasn't ready for this discussion.

Naturally she persisted. "You saved my life. Why?"

With her golden hair, she lit up the night. He lifted her chin, meeting her eyes. "Why do you think?"

Her eyes clouded at his evasion. "I don't know."

He smiled slightly. "Well, maybe when you figure it out, you'll tell me."

Drew wasn't prepared to risk any more than he already had where Olivia was concerned. He could survive a dislocated shoulder, a broken bone or two. But not a broken heart. There would be no going back if either of them made an emotional commitment to their marriage.

Maybe falling in love with Olivia had been pre-ordained, but Drew couldn't be sure of her—not until Jared came home. If their relationship survived her brother's disapproval, they had a future together. Despite his uncertainty, he held her. With his injured arm in a sling, he couldn't make love to her, yet he'd never felt closer to a living soul.

He slept late the following morning.

Olivia brought him breakfast on a tray. "I thought you might be hungry."

He sat up expectantly. "Thanks." After a brief examination of the colorless contents of the tray—cream of rice, toast and tea—his mood sank. He picked up a spoon.

"You've been sleeping for hours." Olivia plumped up the pillow, then tucked an ice pack under his injured shoulder.

It was freezing, but he didn't complain.

She adjusted it. "It's to reduce the swelling."

He swallowed a mouthful of cereal, then set the spoon aside.

Glancing at the uneaten food a moment later, she said, "You've hardly touched your breakfast."

"Olivia," he said patiently, "this stuff tastes like baby food. My shoulder's out of commission. There's nothing wrong with my stomach. Now, can I have some real food? How about ham and eggs and coffee?"

"I'm sorry, but the doctor ordered a light diet." She leaned over him to get the tray. "Maybe a soft-boiled egg?"

Shaking his head, Drew reached for her. Caught off balance, Olivia fell across his lap. "Let's forget about the food," he said huskily, making his intentions clear when he ran his hand down her spine.

She resisted for a moment. "But what about your shoulder?"

Unable to disguise his desperate need for her, he ignored the burning pain. "Let me worry about my shoulder."

Her eyes darkened. "Do you believe in fate? That there's one special person meant for another?"

"Soul mates?" This was no time for a lengthy discussion.

"Something like that."

Drew couldn't hide behind lies.

"I believe in you," he said, realizing it for the first time. Without conscious thought, he'd put his faith in her. With her at his side, anything seemed possible. "Do we need to put it into words? Isn't it enough to feel this?"

He slid his hand under the hem of her flannel shirt—his shirt…his woman. For the first time in his life, he felt more than an urge to possess.

She was part of him.

Olivia felt a shiver of excitement as she always did when he touched her. But was it enough? She stopped thinking when his mouth found hers. Opening to his invasion, she felt like sinking into him. Without releasing her mouth, he rolled over, carrying her with him. He groaned when she unbuttoned his shirt, sifting her hands through the dark hair on his chest.

Sitting up, she removed her own shirt. Her nipples puckered in the cool air, then his hand warmed her. Getting him out of his jeans proved a more difficult feat. He smiled at her blushes. She'd never undressed a man. At first she felt awkward; but by the time she finished, they were both fully aroused.

As she leaned over him, the sunlight touched every inch of her. To Drew, in that moment she seemed golden. Without saying a word, she came to him. With every move, his injured arm ached. But other parts of his body ached more.

The agony was worth the ecstasy of loving Olivia.

Chapter Fourteen

Eventually they got around to sharing a light breakfast. Drew ate his soft-boiled egg without comment. After they finished eating, Olivia removed the tray, then carried it downstairs. She washed the dishes and neatly stored them away.

Overhead she heard the shower running. When it stopped, she went back to the bedroom and found Drew half-dressed.

So he was going to be stubborn.

He'd removed his sling. A white bandage covered the surgical incision on his shoulder.

With a sigh, Olivia sat on the edge of the bed and watched him awkwardly struggle to get his left arm into the sleeve of a plaid shirt. "What are you doing?" she asked after a few minutes of this.

He glanced at her. "Getting dressed for work. I

can still get in a few hours at the mill, do some paperwork.''

She frowned in disapproval. ''But Dr. Peterson advised a couple of days of inactivity.''

''I'm fine,'' he said. In fact, he looked better than fine.

He looked downright sexy. He'd finally managed to get his shirt on, but the front remained unbuttoned, revealing a wide muscled expanse of chest.

With a pain-filled wince, he slipped his arm back into the sling. He looked around, then in the closet. ''Have you seen my boots? Did I leave them downstairs?''

Last night while he slept, Olivia had removed them and placed them at the bedside. With the heel of her foot, she slid them farther under the bed. Determined to make him follow doctor's orders, she tried to look innocent. ''What boots?''

''My work boots,'' he said patiently.

She folded her arms. ''You don't need them. There's no reason for you to rush back to work. I checked with Abby. They can manage without you for a couple of days.''

Drew raised an eyebrow. ''Exactly who's in charge over there?''

''You are, of course. You can get in touch with Abby by phone. This is only a temporary arrangement. Jack is working at the landing and trucking the logs to the sawmill.''

Olivia had neatly arranged everything.

Drew should have felt relieved; instead, he had to acknowledge a sense of chagrin. His injury was a major calamity to him, but only a minor setback to everyone else. So much for his bruised ego. Was that

all that was hurting? The answer was fairly obvious.
Olivia didn't need him.

On the surface, she was warm, but it was all part
of her act. Underneath the charm, Olivia was holding
back, protecting herself from hurt. He couldn't really
blame her. She'd had a shabby childhood. His parents had spoiled him; they might not always have
understood him, but he'd always felt loved.

He admired Olivia for surviving the instability of
her background. She was independent, maddeningly
so at times. He wondered if he would ever really
know her. Nevertheless, she aroused all his protective instincts.

Apparently trying to reassure him, Olivia said,
"Abby promised to contact you if anything comes
up."

Although uncomfortable, Drew had to accept the
fact that he wasn't desperately needed. Besides, he
had little choice but to stay home and follow the
doctor's orders.

Olivia had hidden his boots.

She was kind enough, however, to button his shirt
when he insisted on getting dressed.

"I have no intention of spending the day in bed.
That is, unless you care to join me..." He placed his
free hand on her waist.

"Sorry, I have to get back to work." With a soft
smile to lessen the rejection, she fastened the last
button of his shirt.

"I'd rather be taking it off," he said huskily, then
dropped a kiss on her startled mouth.

Her eyes teased him. "Maybe later."

He laughed. "Is that a promise?"

"Yes."

* * *

That evening, Fred stopped by with a food offering.

Drew stared at the wicker basket. "I hope there's something red and raw in there."

"Nope. Chicken soup."

Drew groaned. "I was hoping for a thick juicy steak."

Olivia accepted the basket, examining the contents with smiling approval. "The doctor ordered a light diet."

Nodding sagely, Fred took a seat at the table. "Never argue with a woman when she's playing nursemaid. It's a losing battle. Just sit back and enjoy it."

That was a tall order.

Drew couldn't relax. Apart from the frustration of being close to Olivia, wanting her with every breath, yet unable to do anything about it, he was itching to get back to work. With work at the sawmill getting under way, he couldn't afford to let things slide. For the first time in his life, he had something—and someone—to lose.

"Wife's gone to her church meeting. I haven't had a good game of cribbage since Ira passed away," Fred said, gesturing at the game board. "You up to it?"

Conscious of the extended olive branch, Drew nodded. "How about a refresher course on the rules?"

Fred chuckled. "Never had much use for them. But if we had a little music, that would be just about perfect."

"I'll find something." Olivia dug out Ira's favorite collection of Scottish tunes.

As the music rose, an odd peace settled over the room.

Olivia sat and worked on a commissioned piece. Her canvas was a large piece of heavy cotton stretched on a wood frame.

Drew watched a colorful winter village scene come to life under her hands. The oval rug wasn't large, but the details were exquisite. It was an idyllic New England winter setting—a skating pond surrounded by skeletal trees. She was currently adding a wreathlike green border.

Drew tried to keep his mind on Fred's instructions, but his gaze kept straying to Olivia, head bent over her work.

With precision, she selected a green strip of wool, placed it into a hooklike tool that she pushed through the cotton backing. After pulling the strip through, she carefully clipped the ends to make the pile plush and even. She seemed thoroughly absorbed.

But when she looked up and caught him staring, their eyes locked and he discovered she wasn't quite as detached as she seemed. He smiled and she blushed...and Fred pretended not to notice.

"Do you skate?" Drew asked idly, more interested in the way the soft rose color climbed in her cheeks.

She shook her head. "Not on ice. Only on rollers."

Making plans for their future, Drew said, "I'll teach you to ice-skate. The pond should freeze up soon."

With the reminder of winter, he shook off a sense

of unease, choosing, instead, to take each day as it came.

However, a chill warning encased his heart.

Fred called Drew's attention back to the game. The evening wore on. Drew concentrated on his strategy, playing and discarding cards as he moved his peg around the holes to victory.

They were tied, ten games each, when Fred said, "One more game to break the tie?"

A competitive edge kicked in as Drew accepted the challenge. He stared at his cards—three fives, a jack of diamonds and two scrub cards. He needed a five of diamonds for a total of twenty-nine—a magic hand. The Super Bowl of hands.

Apparently Olivia felt his tension. She set her frame aside, then came to stand behind his chair. He felt her hand light on his shoulder.

Fred cut the deck. Aware that his chances of getting a perfect hand were slim, if not impossible, Drew turned over the cut card. He stared at the five of diamonds.

Fred shook his head in amazement. "I've been playing the game all my life. I've never seen a perfect score!" Forgetting Drew's injury, he slapped Drew on the back.

Still grinning, Drew stifled a pain-filled groan. Adding to his discomfort, Olivia kissed him on the mouth. He wanted her so badly! Would he get to keep her? Like fate, twenty-nine was a fickle number.

Lucky at cards, unlucky at love?

The following morning, Olivia didn't argue when Drew insisted on going to work. He fixed her with a determined look.

"I'm going in to the sawmill." He slipped his forearm out of the sling, flexing his hand. "I can't afford time off just now. I have a customer coming in from out of town today."

"Oh?" She responded in a noncommittal voice. "Someone important?" She picked up his clothes from where he'd left them the day before—on the floor.

He set his hands on his hips. "That depends on your definition. He operates a small company that manufactures wooden lawn furniture. If we can work things out, he's interested in setting up business in Henderson."

She checked the pockets of his jeans for loose change and came up with a quarter and two dimes. "That sounds wonderful."

"Don't get your hopes up."

She wasn't listening. With his jeans wrapped in a ball, ready to toss into the laundry hamper, she said, "I'll just throw some things in to wash, then I'll drive you to the mill. I can stay and help Abby with some paperwork."

"Does that mean I get my boots back?"

She smiled. "Yes."

As it turned out, Drew's morning appointment with the customer went well. The outlook for more work looked promising.

Later Jack stopped in. Abby bristled at his arrival. He called her Abigail, which she obviously resented. Drew found their feud vaguely amusing.

"Abby just ordered lunch from the diner," Drew said. "She ordered extra portions of everything. How about it?"

So Jack stayed for lunch.

Drew's office was crowded by the time Seth arrived. "I heard you were up and around. I just dropped by to see how you were doing."

Olivia propped herself on the arm of Drew's chair. "He'll be fine, as long as he doesn't overdo it."

Seth chuckled. "I didn't realize the accident affected his voice." He reached for a Coke, nodding toward Olivia. "Looks like a keeper to me."

Drew couldn't contain a smile. "She is."

When Reggie LaRoche arrived, the office had a partylike atmosphere. He looked a little awkward at first—until Abby offered him a sandwich and a Coke. "Thanks," he murmured.

"What's up?" Drew asked.

Reggie took an empty chair. "Thing is...I heard about the accident. Heard you might be laid up for a while." He came to the point. "I thought maybe you could use some help. And I could use some work closer to home, so if you've got work, I'll show up. I've got a wife and family...kids wanting to go off to college before long."

Drew didn't hesitate. Until now, he'd been fighting an uphill battle to convince people he was reliable. Maybe he should have taken a dive under a falling tree a lot sooner.

Drew hired Reggie on the spot. "I need someone to finish the job at Stone's End. When can you start?"

Reggie grinned. "Soon as I can get a crew together. I'd sooner sell the logs locally, instead of trucking them a distance."

"Then it's settled."

In the next few days, Reggie LaRoche was only the first applicant. As promised, he rounded up a crew, and work began to run on schedule. There were some adjustments, but few problems.

Drew was relieved when Reggie and his men accepted Jack at face value. Jack was a wild card—in more ways than one. He worked hard and kept to himself.

Jack had little actual logging experience, but was willing to learn, which earned the other men's respect. Loggers were generally a forgiving lot. They judged a man on the strength of his efforts, not the length of his pedigree, which was fortunate for Jack, because he was long on one and short on the other.

Despite the differences in their backgrounds, Drew shared a bond with Jack. They were both overdue for a bit of luck.

Since the accident and the turnaround in his business, Drew had discovered something about himself. He couldn't just cut down Olivia's trees and take from Stone's End.

He had to give something back.

A few days later, when Olivia was out, he was presented with an opportunity to do just that. He sought out Rita Morales in the workroom. Since learning of Rita's deafness, he'd learned some basic signs. Combined with her ability to lip-read, they were able to communicate without too much difficulty.

After greeting her, Drew got straight to the point. "Olivia is sad about cutting the trees down."

"Yes, this is hard for her. And you, I think." Rita smiled sympathetically. "But marriage is good for her. She has her brother and his family, but that is not enough for Olivia. She was lonely before you came.''

Drew smiled, grateful for the kind words. ''I have a plan, but I need your help.''

She frowned, clearly puzzled. ''If I can help, I will. What is this plan?''

With Rita's assistance, Drew enlisted her husband's help. As a result, a large flatbed truck stopped at Stone's End a few days later....

With a wide smile, Ramon handed Olivia an invoice. ''Where do you want me to unload these?''

Olivia stared down at the order for a hundred spruce trees, two-foot seedlings. ''There must be some mistake. We didn't order these.''

Drew looked over her shoulder. ''Yes, we did.''

''I don't understand.'' Olivia turned and frowned at Drew. ''What are we going to do with a hundred trees?''

''Plant them and watch them grow into Christmas trees.'' He kissed her surprised mouth. ''What else?''

A smile grew. She couldn't hide her delight. ''Why didn't you tell me?''

Her reaction was exactly what he'd hoped for. ''I wanted to surprise you.'' He added more seriously, ''Even after we cut some timber, the farm could use a renewable resource. This seemed like a good idea.''

''A Christmas tree farm. I love it.'' Olivia held back, unable to say the words to express her emotions. She loved Drew. It was so new. So fragile. She glanced at the spruce trees in the truck. The seedlings were no more than two feet tall.

But they would grow...and grow.

''Thank you. I never expected anything like this.'' She didn't know what else to say. She'd received

so few gifts in her life. Once, she'd desperately
wanted a doll for her birthday. But she'd known her
mother would forget and so she'd saved up enough
cereal box tops to get it for herself. Like a wounded
child, she'd kept her heart hidden. She'd played at
life, but she'd always played safe. Drew was changing all the rules.

What if there was such a thing as happily-ever-
after?

The spruce trees were planted just in time, before
the frost reached too deeply into the ground.

Before Thanksgiving, Drew distributed turkeys to
everyone who worked for him. It was his way of
saying thanks and starting a new tradition.

Drew's sling came off in time to carve the turkey
on Thanksgiving Day. He looked at the people seated
around him—Abby, Seth and Jack. And Olivia. She
beamed at him from the opposite end of the table.

He wondered if she knew that love shone from her
eyes. She'd never said the words, but he felt it in her
touch, her smile. All the things she didn't say. He
wondered if he was worthy of that gift. He had a lot
to celebrate—his marriage, the launch of the mill.
He'd met with some resistance, but most people had
given him a second chance.

Swallowing hard, he said grace. It was a prayer of
gratitude for a plentiful bounty, and family and
friends to share them with. He added a silent communication, thanking God for Olivia.

"Amen."

He met Olivia's soft gaze, aware that she could
read his thoughts. He didn't mind. He loved her. He

had nothing to hide. For the first time in a long time, he could look with pride on his present life, rather than looking back to where he'd been. Today was for giving thanks.

Tomorrow was filled with promise.

Olivia had been cooking for days. Turkey and stuffing competed for space on the broad oak table with mashed potatoes and gravy, stuffed acorn squash and cranberry relish. And that was just the main course. Side dishes filled with vegetables and rolls accompanied the meal. Then there was dessert—traditional pumpkin, cherry and deep-dish apple pie, and a not-so-common chocolate cheesecake topped with sour cream and bittersweet chocolate curls.

Drew smiled. "All right, who wants a drumstick?"

"I'll take one," Seth said promptly. "And some dressing on the side. What kind is it?"

"Cornbread stuffing," Olivia said, knowing that she would always remember every detail of this day.

"Everything's delicious," Abby said after sampling several dishes. "Where did you learn to cook like this?"

"I worked at a restaurant, the Blue Lagoon, and the cook was a good friend. Actually it's where Jared found me."

The words brought it all back to Olivia. She'd come so far to get to this place. Jared had brought her home. She owed him so much! She and Drew were making their own family traditions, surrounded by friends—even though they were an odd assortment.

She'd invited Fred and his wife, but they were

spending the holiday at a large family reunion. Ramon had accepted a turkey with some reluctance—but he hadn't turned it down. He'd agreed to stay on at Stone's End. Everything was perfect.

Well, almost perfect.

Jessie had called to wish them Happy Thanksgiving.

Not a word from Jared.

Olivia tried to put that out of her mind. Hopefully, in time, Jared would approve of Drew as her choice.

The conversation grew lively, providing a distraction.

Typically Jack didn't have much to say, Olivia noted. He sat on one side of the table, opposite Abby and Seth. Although outwardly relaxed, he seemed tense in this sort of social situation. He never spoke of family. Olivia suspected he didn't have any.

Through course after course, Jack ate, spoke when spoken to and generally kept his opinions to himself. He seemed so alone. Despite that, something about Jack Slade didn't invite pity.

After dinner, Jack offered to help clear the table. So did Abby. "Here, let me." They both reached for the same plate.

Jack's hand brushed Abby's wrist. "Sorry, Abigail," he said in a mocking tone.

"My name is Abby." As if scorched, she released the plate.

Abby turned away, her face flushed as she reached for another dish.

Observing the interaction, Seth frowned when his cell phone went off. "I have to go," he said after taking the call.

"I hope it's nothing serious," Olivia said.

"A snowmobile accident. No one's seriously hurt, but I have to get over there and sort things out."

Abby moved toward him. "I'll get my coat."

Seth reached for his jacket. "There's no need to cut the evening short. Besides, I'm going in the opposite direction."

To everyone's surprise, Jack spoke up. "I can take her home."

Abby bit her lip. "That's very kind of you, but I wouldn't dream of putting you to so much trouble."

"No trouble," Jack replied.

Abby turned to Seth, who merely said, "Sounds good to me. I'll call you later." He fixed Jack with a hard warning look, however, and added, "Just to see that you got home safely."

"Oh, dear," Olivia murmured to Drew, out of earshot of their two remaining guests after Seth had left. "Is there something going on between Jack and Abby?"

Drew chuckled. "It's called instant hate."

"I'd hate for anything to go wrong. Seth loves her. He's been so patient."

"I don't understand how he can wait so long for Abby to make up her mind." That kind of patience was foreign to Drew, who had acted purely on instinct when it came to Olivia. "A little competition might be exactly what Seth needs. He knows what he wants. He just hasn't figured out how to get it."

"And he wants Abby."

Drew shrugged. "Let's forget about Abby and Seth. They have to sort out their own problems."

"And Jack?"

"Don't feel sorry for Jack—he wouldn't thank you for it. Besides, Jack can take care of himself."

* * *

Later, after everyone had left, Drew turned off the lights before going upstairs. Olivia had already gone ahead.

In the bathroom, he ducked under the dainty feminine bits and pieces strung up and scattered around. A delicate white lace teddy was draped over his towel. The scent of her perfume filled the air with her soft fragrance.

He breathed it in, unable to restrain a smile.

He soon discovered the trail she'd left on the way to the bedroom—damp footprints pointed the way. Her flannel nightgown lay draped at the foot of the bed. It was all part of the feminine package that so intrigued him.

Olivia.

The room was dimly lit—a small light cast a halo over her golden head on the pillow. His wayward angel.

He lifted the covers and climbed into bed beside her.

"Are you tired?" he said when she turned to him.

She smiled a siren's smile. "No. Are you?"

The curve of her breast fit into the palm of his hand. "You've been cooking all day," he said, dropping a kiss onto the silky skin of her shoulder.

"I enjoyed every minute. The day was perfect."

He smiled wickedly. "And the best is yet to come."

It was said lightly, and she took it as such. His kiss smothered her soft laugh.

Promises, promises.

Some to keep...and some to break.

Chapter Fifteen

"Jared!"

Olivia couldn't hide her shock—or her dismay—at her brother's arrival the following morning.

Regretting the recent strain between them, she greeted him awkwardly. "I wasn't expecting you for weeks—not before Christmas."

"It's good to see you." He hugged her, his arms strong.

He was a man to lean on, but Olivia didn't want or need a crutch—a fact that he often overlooked. He stepped back with a steely look. Fair-haired and gray-eyed, there was nothing soft about Jared Carlisle.

Jared's smile didn't hide his tension. "I had a break and decided to drive up and see how things are going."

"I'm glad you came." She looked past him, disappointed to see he was alone. "Where are Rachel and the children?"

"Rachel's aunt and uncle are visiting for a couple of weeks. She hasn't seen them in a while, so they're catching up. Rachel sends her love." He looked around. "So where is he?"

"Drew left for work a short while ago. I'm sorry you missed him. You look tired."

He shrugged. "It's a long drive. I could use a cup of coffee if you've got a pot going."

Jared helped himself to a cup and brought her one, as well, reminding Olivia that he'd grown up in this house. He'd had a new house built next to his veterinary clinic, but she supposed this house would always be a part of him. She didn't mind sharing it with him or with Jessie.

"I passed a logging site on the way here," he said once they'd settled at the table. "In one of our phone calls, you mentioned that Drew was reopening the sawmill, but not that he's hauling wood out of Stone's End."

Olivia defended her decision. "I'm sorry if you don't approve, but I really don't see how it concerns you."

"Perhaps not. But you concern me, Olivia. I wanted to come sooner, immediately after I heard about you and Drew getting married. But Rachel talked me into waiting and giving the marriage a chance. Now I wish I hadn't waited."

"What do you mean?"

He looked at her with obvious pity. "Apart from the logging operation, I heard there was some trouble last week. Something about Drew tangling with a tree."

"It was a minor accident," Olivia admitted.

"Minor?" His mouth thinned, revealing his uncompromising side. "I heard you were almost killed. If that's the way Drew is looking after you and Stone's End, I'd hate to be on the receiving end when things really start to go wrong."

"Drew was hurt while trying to save me." Olivia stared at her brother in frustration. "It was entirely my fault, not Drew's. Why can't I convince you of that? Why does everyone always assume the worst about him?"

"Maybe because they've got good reason."

Olivia stood up. "He's been nothing but kind to me."

"Kind?" Jared laughed harshly. "Drew doesn't know the meaning of the word."

"I appreciate your concern," she said, picking up her cup and taking it to the kitchen sink. "But I can't live my life to please you."

"I'd give anything to be wrong about Drew," he said. "Unfortunately I haven't seen or heard anything around here to relieve my suspicions."

Olivia's heart skipped as she turned to face her brother. "What suspicions?"

"There are some things you should know."

With a sigh, Olivia said, "I know about the explosion and all about Drew's past. He's never tried to hide or make excuses for his mistakes or pretend to be anything but what he is."

Jared met her troubled gaze. "And none of it bothers you?"

"Yes, of course, it bothers me. But he's tried so hard to put it behind him. Don't you think he deserves a second chance? People in town are beginning to trust him. They're coming back to work at the sawmill. He's earned that the hard way.''

Jared released a breath. ''All right, I'll admit he seems to be making a go of the sawmill. But I'm more concerned about your marriage. Do you trust him?''

''Yes,'' she said firmly. ''I know everything I need to know about Drew.''

''Do you?''

Jared's gray eyes pierced hers. He reminded her of Ira in that moment. Olivia felt the bonds of family tightening around her. ''Yes, I know him. I'm his wife.''

''And you think that makes the difference? Do you know everything about Drew,'' he demanded, ''or simply what he's chosen to tell you?''

She sighed. ''What else is there to tell?''

''I don't need to rake up every detail of Drew's misbegotten past. There's only one thing you really need to know.'' Jared's eyes softened. ''He used you, just as he once tried to use Jessie. He was determined to marry a Carlisle with the aim of acquiring the farm's valuable timber rights.''

''He wanted to marry Jessie for the farm?''

''I'm sorry, but it's true. You played right into his hands.''

Jared continued to speak, but she didn't hear a word. Out of all the chaotic thoughts, only one thing was clear to Olivia. Jared had never lied to her.

Later Drew walked into the house and found the kitchen cluttered with pots and pans. Immediately he knew something was up with Olivia. In the short time they'd been married, he'd learned one thing about his bride. Strong emotion fired her creative culinary talents.

Whenever she was glad or mad or sad, she cooked.

Drew looked at a bag of flour spilling its contents onto the kitchen counter and wondered which mood Olivia was expressing now. He greeted her with a wary smile.

She looked pale and hollow-eyed. She was adding cubed butternut squash to a casserole dish.

"Jared's here," she announced in a tight voice.

Her tone said it all. Drew was in trouble.

A cold feeling of dread swept over him. "I saw his car when I passed his house. What's up?" The words were a deliberate attempt to sound casual, but Drew couldn't summon a smile.

"He's only going to be in town for a few days. He was here earlier." She added corn syrup and pecans to the mix. "He was exhausted after the long drive. He went home, but he promised to come for breakfast in the morning."

Drew was grateful for the delay in facing Jared. Hopefully, that would give him time for a little damage control.

He leaned against the counter. "I thought he wasn't due for another few weeks. Why the change in plans?"

Turning to him, Olivia wiped her hands on a towel. "He heard about the accident and was concerned."

"The accident happened more than a week ago," Drew said with cool smile. "It's old news."

"Yes, well, he wanted to come sooner, but this was the earliest he could get away. He has to get back to the university by the middle of next week."

"So he just came by to check up on your health?"

"And yours," she inserted. "He's concerned."

Drew said in disbelief. "Is that why you're upset?"

With a shrug, she turned, back to the squash. "I'm not upset," she said in a very small voice. "Anyway, I'd rather not discuss it."

She tossed an apple into the blender and flipped the switch to the "on" position. The grinding noise effectively cut off conversation—but not for long.

Drew reached around and flipped it off. "Damn it! Look at me! What else did he say?"

She spun around. "I think you know."

The shimmering brightness of unshed tears swimming in her gray eyes almost undid Drew. But there could be no more evasions. He'd always known the day of reckoning would come. He'd just hoped for more time. Now time had run out. With a deep sigh, he placed a hand on either side of her waist, trapping her so she couldn't escape.

"No more evasions." He spoke directly. "I gather all this has something to do with me. Something unflattering, no doubt."

Like a dam breaking, the words rushed out of her. "It's not just about you. It's about you and my sister, Jessie."

With a flinch that betrayed his guilt, Drew took the blow. He forced himself to ask, "Exactly what did he say?"

She searched his eyes. He wondered if she could see to the depths of his soul. "He said you wanted to marry Jessie at one time."

He tried to explain. "We weren't that involved.

Most of the time, she wouldn't even speak to me. That's about it.''

"Oh, God.'' She rubbed a hand across her brow.

Drew asked, "What else did Jared say?''

"Isn't that enough?'' Faced with the awful facts, Olivia obviously wanted him to deny Jared's accusations.

He didn't even try. "I imagine there's more.''

They stood close. He felt her breasts rise and fall against his chest as she said, "He also said you wanted to marry Jessie for the timber rights to Stone's End—that you'd do anything to get your hands on them.''

Drew said quietly, "And you believed him?''

She hesitated a long moment, then whispered, "If it's not true, then tell me it's a lie.''

She'd obviously made her choice.

"I can't,'' he admitted, and watched her face close up, like a delicate blossom out of the sun's rays. To his shame, he'd gone along with Ira's plans. He gave her a moment to digest his admission. "But I'm not that same man.'' He ground the words out. "And aren't you forgetting one small fact? You proposed to *me,* remember?''

She shook her head, obviously trying to deny him. "Why didn't you tell me about you and Jessie?''

"I tried—almost from the very beginning. You said nothing would change your mind about me. You don't know how many times I came so close to telling you.''

Her shuttered face told Drew all he needed to know.

"I wish you had,'' she whispered.

"So do I.''

* * *

Later in bed, Olivia whispered, "Good night."

Drew felt her coldness. He stared into the darkness and felt it closing in on him. Surely there was some solution, some explanation to make all this go away. "We should talk."

With a note of desperation breaking in her voice, she whispered back, "Please, not now."

He died a little inside when she turned away.

Her reaction simply reinforced his general impression. He suspected that only Olivia's pride and her stubborn refusal to admit she'd made a mistake was preventing her from throwing him out and ending their brief marriage. She'd let him stay, refusing to admit failure, which was just like her.

Drew ought to be grateful, but he wasn't. He felt betrayed. Their entire marriage was built on a weak foundation. Love had been a possibility, never a reality with any substance.

Once the flaws were exposed, their relationship would only continue to erode until there was nothing left.

She was all shiny and new, and he was all used up—five years of his life spent locked away. Loving Olivia had meant risking both his heart and his pride when he had so little left of both. He'd gambled on love and lost.

The following morning, the emotional storm swirled around them. Drew could feel it pulling them apart. Olivia was a pale reflection of the radiant woman he'd married.

Breakfast was strained. Jared and Olivia hardly said a word beyond, "Please pass the toast," and, "Thank you."

Drew said nothing at all. He felt like the unwelcome guest at a funeral. Clearly he was the outsider. He didn't belong at Stone's End.

Jared finally addressed him with a terse, "Drew, it's been a while."

"Olivia tells me that you and Rachel have quite a family."

Despite his obvious impatience with the entire situation, Jared smiled. "They're great."

"I never pictured you with a brood of kids."

"Goes to show how some things can change. And some things don't." The jab was indirect.

Nevertheless, Drew felt it. "But you don't think I've changed, is that it?"

"That's it."

Drew couldn't avoid the challenge. "I know your opinion of me is pretty low at this point, and maybe I earned that in the past. But I think I can make Olivia happy."

Jared snapped. "How long do you think that will last?"

Drew waited for Olivia to rise to his defense.

Instead, she stood up and silenced them both with a few heated words. "Please, just stop it! I don't want to discuss this again. We've been over and over it. I married Drew, and that's all there is to it."

Somehow Drew didn't feel that was much of an endorsement.

Olivia and her brother were barely speaking, and Drew could see that it was eating her up inside. After destroying his own family, he couldn't bear to stand back and watch the same thing happen to the Carlisles. No matter how he tried to avoid the truth, he knew he was single-handedly destroying the one thing Olivia cared about most—her family.

Drew would only hurt her by staying.

Clearly, Olivia couldn't make the choice, so Drew made it for her. There was only one solution. He had to leave.

Far better to make a clean break. There was no point in dragging things out.

He left without finishing his breakfast.

After Drew left, Olivia stared at his empty chair, the cold remnants of a ham-and-cheese omelet on his plate. She'd made poppy-seed muffins—which he hadn't touched. In times of stress, cooking always calmed her, but today it did nothing to soothe the ache in her heart. She felt cold, and wondered if she'd ever feel warm again.

So it was true.

According to Jared, Drew had taken advantage of her innocence and her family's absence to secure his long-held ambition. And Olivia had handed Stone's End to him on a silver platter—along with herself, body and soul. She couldn't bear to think of that just now. There would be time for tears later.

She'd prayed that Jared was wrong, that Drew would have a reasonable explanation. But he hadn't even tried to defend himself against her brother's accusations.

He hadn't kissed her before he left.

She wanted to run after him, but the weight of all her insecurities kept her there. She'd fallen for the oldest con game in the book. She'd almost believed in love.

In one way or another, life had taught Olivia some pretty tough lessons. Well, here was one more to add to the list. How could she have trusted Drew? He'd wanted the farm, not her. He'd never denied his willingness to go to any lengths to get Stone's End—including marrying Jessie—or her.

Apparently any old Carlisle would do.

Olivia's heart turned cold.

How could she have fooled herself into thinking Drew could love her for herself?

Oh, she'd thought she was immune to men and the sweet lies they told. But it seemed she'd inherited her mother's weakness, after all. She'd put all her faith in Drew, and he'd betrayed her. Olivia smiled sadly.

Why did she marry him so blindly? Why was she so impulsive? In the end, she had only herself to blame; Drew had tried to warn her. All the signs were there, but she'd refused to read them. From the first, Drew had wanted Stone's End, not her. She'd proposed marriage and gotten exactly what she wanted.

Why was she so hurt?

At the sawmill, Drew wasted no time taking care of unfinished business and cleaning out some items from his desk.

Abby watched in total dismay. "You can't just leave."

His smile twisted. "Abby, this has nothing to do with you. But you were absolutely right. I made a mistake marrying Olivia. I'm merely trying to make repairs." He'd always taken what he wanted in life without counting the cost to anyone—even himself. This time, he couldn't do it. Olivia's happiness came first.

"I don't want to be right," she said, revealing her deep concern and frustration with the situation. "I want you to stay. You know you love Olivia. She loves you."

He opened a small safe and took out an envelope, then handed it to Abby. "She loves her family more."

Abby stared down at the envelope. "What's this?"

"The deeds to the sawmill and Stone's End. I want Olivia to have it all." Things at the sawmill were going smoothly. No one really needed him.

"Aren't you going to tell her?"

"I included a note. She'll understand."

He hoped she'd understand that it was best this way. If he saw her again, he might weaken. She'd only try to stop him from doing what they both knew he had to do—walk away from her and Henderson. He never should have come back, never should have stayed. He'd been looking for something or someone, trying to piece the fragments of his life together. It was just Olivia's bad luck that they'd run into each other.

For a brief time, he'd thought he'd found all the missing parts, a future with Olivia, but he'd been proved wrong. He had only himself to blame for expecting too much. In the end, Olivia's faith in him was tested to the breaking point.

And it broke.

The conflict would inevitably destroy the family she'd found so late and loved so deeply. Drew had to leave and give her the deed to both properties. It was the first unselfish act in his life. That was how much he loved Olivia. Better to cut his losses now. There were other towns, other jobs—one was just the same as the next. But none of them had Olivia.

Abby said quietly, "Please don't do this."

Drew took a deep breath. "I'll be in touch as soon as I know where I'm going." He smiled wryly at the words. So much for the new stable image. "Can you see that Olivia gets my message after I'm gone?"

Although visibly upset, Abby agreed.

An hour later, Drew wasn't surprised when Abby wasn't around to say goodbye. In fact, he was relieved. The last thing he wanted was a protracted, emotional farewell.

He'd written Olivia a note, telling her he was sorry.

That was it.

What more could he say? That his heart was ripped in two, that he was leaving it behind, that he'd never feel whole again without her? Of course, he couldn't say any of those things.

So he walked out, taking only what he'd come with, which was nothing. He'd come to Olivia empty-handed with nothing to offer but his heart. It was in her keeping for as long as she wanted it. He didn't need it anymore.

Olivia was filling some Christmas orders when her sister-in-law arrived. Abby hesitated when she saw the full house.

"I hope I'm not interrupting."

"Not at all," Olivia assured her. "Please come in. Rita and I were just boxing up these rugs. We could use a break."

Abby greeted Jared with some reservation. She warmed up a bit and smiled at Rita Morales. "Hello again." And Fred earned an even warmer, "It's good to see you."

When Olivia offered to make a pot of fresh coffee,

Abby said, "Oh, please don't. I can't stay long. If you have a few minutes, I was hoping to talk to you."

No one took the obvious hint to give them some privacy.

Fred said, "That's okay, we're all family."

The words startled Olivia. She looked around and realized this was her family—Jared had come all the way from New York because he was worried about her, Fred and Rita were showing their support, and Abby was interfering because she genuinely cared. Olivia didn't have to face this crisis alone.

Why had it taken her so long to see that truth?

Independent and wary of close family ties, she'd found it hard to fit into the Carlisle family. Ira had accepted her without question. Jared and Jessie were as close to her as a brother and sister could possibly be.

They'd all tried to bring Olivia into the family circle; but their memories weren't hers. And nothing could ever change the years they'd spent apart. Or give her a sense of a complete family. She'd nursed the wounds too long. It was time to let go and move on.

To come inside her family's circle.

"Fred's right," Olivia said, shaping the words as they settled in her heart. "We're all family."

Abby's eyes were still troubled. "I'm not sure I should be doing this, but I had to come." That said, she continued with more determination, "Drew asked me to wait and give you this after he left. But I decided it couldn't wait." She held out a large envelope and a smaller one.

Olivia took the small one first. "What do you mean?"

Abby said, "I'm sorry he didn't tell you himself. All Drew ever wanted was you. He's given up everything, rather than cause more division between you and your family. Do you know how lucky you are to be loved like that?"

Jared defended his sister. "Now wait a minute. Olivia isn't responsible for Drew's decision."

"I tried to talk him out of it, but he insisted his way was best. He left you the deeds to everything." Some of Abby's bitterness spilled out. "Isn't that why you married Drew in the first place? To get Stone's End?"

Olivia found the words. "No, of course not."

Feeling remote, surrounded by friends and family, she opened Drew's letter and read the words scrawled in black across the crisp white paper.

In time, I hope you'll understand why I had to leave. It's for the best. The only thing I regret is never telling you that I loved you.

Drew

Was this how they would end?

Had all the promises come to this?

Olivia recalled the early days when they'd first met. They'd walked by a lake, and anything had seemed possible. The sky was blue, the sun golden, the leaves brilliant, gaudy and beautiful...and then, they were gone. Like love. Hadn't Olivia always known it could be given away or stolen in one reckless moment? She'd given Drew her love—as fragile as an autumn leaf clinging to a tree. One gust of harsh reality had blown it away.

Olivia stared at his bold signature at the bottom of the farewell note. She reread it, until the words were etched on her soul like ice crystals—cold and hard and transparent.

But he'd written that he loved her.

Past tense?

Had she destroyed it?

Chapter Sixteen

Crushing the note in her hand, Olivia looked out the window at the rolling fields and gentle hills surrounding Stone's End—this place that connected her to her family and gave her the roots she'd longed for all her life, this place that seemed so foreign at first. This place called home.

She'd learned to love everything and everyone here. She'd sacrificed her pride to own it.

Had she sacrificed love, as well?

Her eyes filmed with unshed tears. Through them, she saw the newly planted rows of spruce trees—seedlings that would one day grow into a renewable resource for Stone's End, enabling her to have her dream. A tear fell. Drew had given her that dream. If she needed proof of his love, there it was.

The knowledge came too late.

While Olivia stood, trying to sort through her emotions, Jared opened the second envelope to reveal the contents—the official deeds to both Stone's End and the Pierce properties.

With a confused expression, Jared ran a hand though his hair. "He's signed everything over to you," he said, but his suspicion died hard. "What the hell is he up to now?"

"Well…" Fred shook his head in consternation, then pronounced his verdict. "Now we've got a real mess on our hands that needs some straightening out. You know what I always say—"

Olivia interrupted with a bitter "I know, a skunk never sheds its stripes."

With a wounded look, Fred shook his head. "I was going to say—every man deserves a second chance."

"Fred's right," Jared agreed, in a complete about-face. "If these mean anything—" He indicated the legal papers that had engineered Olivia's marriage. "—then I'll grant you, maybe Drew didn't want Stone's End, after all."

After that faint endorsement, Olivia stared at her brother. The Carlisle stubborn streak must be a curse! Jared had inherited it from Ira, and so had Jessie. And Olivia. Rather than risk her heart and let love speak for itself, she'd let her pride come between her and Drew.

Why was it so impossible to accept the simple fact that he loved her? Why had she made such a tangle out of her emotions? At the very moment Drew needed it most, she'd withdrawn her trust, her faith. And what was faith but believing that the impossible was possible? Could she believe in Drew?

First she had to believe in herself.

Apparently Jared had her and Drew all figured out.

"All right, maybe I was wrong about Drew." he said. "Maybe he didn't want Stone's End. The old Drew would never walk out on the prize without so much as putting up a good fight."

"It's much more complicated than that."

Jared sighed. "Then uncomplicate it. Drew might be a lot of things, but he's no quitter. Even I know that much about him. Maybe I misjudged him."

"Maybe?" Olivia repeated the obvious understatement in disbelief. "Well, right or wrong, Drew's gone now."

"Look," Jared said. "The guy's obviously crazy about you. The point is, what are you going to do about it?"

Olivia wanted to run and hide and nurse her wounds. "It's too late. Besides, I wouldn't know what to say."

Until then, Rita had been silently observing. Now she said softly, "That is simple." She demonstrated, circling her heart with a closed fist turned outward. "Tell him you are sorry." She smiled gently. "If he loves you, that will be enough."

After taking care of some business at the bank and saying goodbye to Jack and Reggie and a few others, Drew got a later start than he'd intended.

A few morning flurries had turned into an afternoon squall. They were possibly due for a nor'easter, and Drew was hoping to get as far as Presque Isle before it got really bad, hopefully before nightfall. He was almost to the county line when he heard a police siren. A blue light pierced the whitening world around him. Drew checked—no, he wasn't speeding.

He pulled over, relieved when he saw Seth getting out of his car and walking toward him.

Drew climbed out of his car, too. "I'm glad you caught up with me. I was hoping to see you before I left."

Seth said, "And I'm hoping to change your mind about leaving Henderson. You're making a big mistake."

"Look, if Abby sent you, it's too late. I've thought it over and made up my mind." Leaving Henderson was the hardest thing he'd ever had to do in his entire life! And Seth wasn't making it any easier. "I'm doing what I think is best for everyone concerned."

"I think you're wrong about that. There are a lot of people who are counting on you to stay and finish what you started. And I'm not just talking about the sawmill. By the way, Abby didn't send me." Seth confessed, "But I did bring reinforcements."

"Not Olivia!" Drew shot back with a pained grimace that revealed the depth of his emotions.

"No," Seth said. "Jared's with me."

With that brief warning, Drew stiffened when he saw Olivia's brother climb out of the patrol car.

Jared approached, stopping a few feet away. "Olivia got your note," he said coolly, his opinion of Drew's behavior obviously low.

Drew braced himself against the bitter disappointment. "In that case, why isn't she here, instead of you?"

For a moment, Jared looked completely baffled. "Is that what you expected? That she'd come running after you?" He shook his head. "I'll say one thing, you've got a lot of nerve. You're the one who's walking out."

"Just to set the record straight," Drew bit out, finally losing his temper. "I never asked for anything from Olivia that she wasn't prepared to give. And I wouldn't be fool enough to leave if I thought there was a chance in hell that she wanted me to stay! Does that answer your question?"

Jared smiled. "Yes, it does."

The smile infuriated Drew. "Don't look so damn smug!"

"I can't help it. If you feel that way about Olivia, why the farewell note? Why not tell her how you feel?"

"Olivia doesn't really want marriage—she never did. I was just a guy who happened along. She wants Stone's End."

"All right, if you say so but I think you could be wrong." With that surprising admission, Jared had another argument. "I shouldn't have interfered between you and Olivia. As a matter of fact, Rachel warned me, but I didn't listen. Anyway, I'm willing to bury the hatchet, if you are."

The offer caught Drew off guard. Nevertheless, he nodded, accepting Jared's apology.

Jared said, "I'm ready to admit that you're the right man for Olivia. Don't you think you owe her more than a scribbled farewell note?"

Drew said dryly, "Do you want it written in blood?"

"No, I simply want my baby sister to be happy—which she isn't at the moment. Plenty of marriages get off to a rocky start—I should know," he added with a smile that revealed more than he probably intended. "But it can be the best thing if you work at it. And if you find the right woman. I don't want

the breakup of Olivia's marriage on my conscience.
Don't you think you owe each other a second
chance?''

"How does Olivia fit into this?"

"She's agreed to meet with you."

Drew slowly absorbed that. Maybe his heart felt
just a little lighter. "Do you realize that if Olivia and
I work things out, that will make the two of us related?''

"Brothers-in-law!" Jared looked as if he was having trouble swallowing that. "I guess I can handle
that. Does that mean you'll give the marriage another
shot?''

Drew wasn't convinced that a last-ditch effort to
salvage his marriage would work. "I think you're
wrong.''

"What do you have to lose?"

Everything.

He'd gambled on Olivia and lost. He'd made so
many mistakes. He'd needed collateral to buy back
the sawmill, and she'd needed a husband to meet the
terms of Ira's will. Then he'd complicated it by falling in love with her.

For some time, he'd known she meant more to him
than a contract, a signature on a piece of paper. But
he hadn't been prepared to accept the strong emotions she aroused in him from that first meeting. He
suspected Olivia had shared his feelings. Afraid love
wouldn't stand the test of time, they'd rushed into
marriage, emotionally challenged, using a financial
partnership as an excuse not to wait. They'd never
given love a chance.

Drew wished he'd understood that a lot sooner.

Was it too late to undo the damage?

Drew was skeptical, yet he wanted Olivia badly enough to try one more time. "All right. You and Seth are obviously working together on this. What's next?"

Drew knew he'd been set up when Jared said, "It's all arranged. You and Olivia meet on neutral ground."

With the temperature below freezing and a fierce wind driving the heavy snowfall, Drew could barely see six feet in front of him by the time he turned down the rough track leading into the woods and the cabin where Olivia had agreed to meet with him, apparently at Jared's suggestion. All around him, the woods were silent, muffled by snow. Every defect, every flaw was hidden. The scene looked so peaceful, so pure.

It mocked the turmoil in his heart.

He didn't want to argue with Olivia; he didn't want to hurt her any more than she'd already been hurt by the facts surrounding their marriage. And what exactly were those facts? He'd married her because he wanted her, but she'd probably never believe that now.

She was obviously convinced he'd only married her in order to get his hands on Stone's End. The thought had never entered his mind, but he could see how his actions might appear suspicious to Jared, Fred and the others. And Olivia.

How could he convince her that he didn't give a damn about anything else? He'd given her the deeds. What more could he give? It had taken every ounce of determination to leave her. Now here he was—right back where they started.

Drew climbed out of the car.

This meeting would only prolong the agony. How many times could he walk away from her? Maybe he wouldn't have to. He opened the door, then walked in.

Olivia stood in the shadows. She clasped her hands behind her back. "I'm glad you came."

She didn't look glad.

In fact, she looked miserable. At the sight of her pale, troubled face and stricken eyes, Drew knew she was there under duress—just as he was. Apparently Jared and Abby, and who knew how many others, had been busy matchmaking.

Taking a minute to collect his thoughts and plan his next move, Drew stomped the snow off his feet. "Jared said you wanted to talk."

Olivia came forward and took his jacket. "I think we should, don't you?"

Drew decided to make things easier for her. "Look, this wasn't my idea. I'm damn sorry about all this. None of this is your fault."

Hugging his jacket to her breast, she said, "Then whose fault is it?"

Trying to control his disappointment, he responded coolly, "Obviously a few of our well-meaning friends and family have decided to play Cupid. They cooked up this ridiculous attempt at reconciliation, but it isn't going to work."

In a very small voice, she said, "It isn't?"

Although they stood only feet apart, he didn't dare reach out and touch her. Her gray eyes were filled with doubt. How much more evidence did he need? "I know Jared is your brother, and he means well."

She wouldn't accept that. "But he shouldn't have interfered."

Drew looked at her in surprise. "He admitted as much. I imagine he tried to convince you there's something left to salvage in our relationship. Some things can't be fixed—and our marriage is one of them." When she said nothing to dispute his version of their relationship, Drew reached the natural conclusion. "I think you'll agree that it's best this way. We can each go our separate ways. You're free."

She was free.

He was free.

To do what?

Wasn't that exactly where they'd started?

Moving away, Olivia set his jacket to dry on the back of a chair near the fire. Snow melted and dripped, steaming when it hit the grate.

"I see," Olivia whispered.

Although each word from his lips had created a deeper chasm, she didn't know how to stop what was happening. Shouldn't the fact that she'd swallowed her pride and come here be enough to end any further talk of his leaving? If Drew loved her, wasn't he supposed to sweep her into his arms, then beg her forgiveness for not telling her about his courtship of Jessie? Instead, he was looking at her as if he didn't like her very much. Maybe she deserved it. Wasn't she the one to break faith?

In that case, she had to make the repairs.

She took a first step toward him. When she moved away from the fire, he noticed the table set with candles and wine, and his voice stopped her. "What kind of game are we playing now?"

Although the cynicism in his eyes almost crushed

her, she stood very straight, reminding herself that she'd helped put it there. "It's no game. I asked Jared to bring you here."

She saw his eyes lift in shock. "You did!"

She nodded. "This was the only way I could think of to stop you from leaving before I had a chance to explain a few things."

He groaned. "There's nothing to explain."

"But there is," she insisted, willing him to listen with his heart. "When I first met you, I was all caught up in breaking my father's will. It was almost a contest—his wishes against mine. All that blinded me to everything else, even you. Then, when we got married, I hid behind the legalities and I never stopped. Because it felt safe."

"How safe?"

She smiled. "Not safe enough, apparently, because I fell in love with you." She watched his eyes darken, but when he didn't say anything, she continued, her confidence faltering just a bit. "After Jared came, I should have listened to what you were trying to tell me. I realize there was never anything between you and Jessie that could possibly threaten what we have now."

To her disappointment, Drew latched on to one point. "I should have told you about Jessie sooner— that was my mistake."

"I'm so sorry for not trusting you. But it really wasn't you. It was me. Can you understand—it was never faith in you that was missing, but faith in myself? I didn't think you could love me."

He sighed. "And I don't know how to convince you."

Setting a lifetime of disappointments aside, Olivia

put every ounce of courage into her voice as she said, "On the note, you said you loved me. Is that true?"

Did he love her?

Of course, Drew knew the answer, but he needed to be sure that Olivia was ready to hear it and accept the new terms of their relationship. From this point, there would be no turning back. He looked at Olivia, hoping to find the answer.

Wearing a pensive frown, she stood by the fireplace, where the flames shed light, playing over her delicate body. She looked small and defenseless. But the same flame that melts butter forges steel.

Reminded of that, Drew knew that Olivia was made of something strong and enduring. He didn't know anything about her mother, but he knew Olivia had inherited her father's strength. She was her father's daughter, which meant that she could be a formidable opponent in any contest, even the game of love.

Did he love her?

His resistance cracked. "Yes, it's true," he said so she would never get confused again. Then he took the next step—she'd come far enough, so he'd meet her halfway. He crossed that room, and the space shrank with each step, each word. And finally he took her in his arms. "I love you more than life," he whispered, against her lips. He crushed her to him, shocked at how close he'd come to losing her. Her mouth was hot and lush and open to him, welcoming him inside.

There were tears in her eyes when he released her. "I was so mixed-up about so many things," she blurted, anxious to erase all their differences; every obstacle fell with each word. "Even Ira. He must have known I was far too stubborn to marry anyone I couldn't love.''

"And I love you," she whispered, her eyes glowing, promising him a world they would create together. She frowned slightly. "There's just one small detail. Did I ever mention the small print in the will?"

Drew groaned, "More conditions?"

"Mmm." Her eyes shining with hope and faith, Olivia described the terms. "We have to stay married for fifty years, maybe more," she said solemnly while her eyes offered untold delights. "And we have to have lots and lots of children."

Sweet, sweet lies.

Drew just smiled. "Good old Ira."

Olivia smiled back. "I think he would approve, don't you?"

Recognizing the importance of his response, Drew said, "I know he would. If the will is what it took, then I have Ira to thank for you." When she smiled, he murmured huskily, "I love you."

Sometimes, a man has to wander far to find his way home. And sometimes, he has to lose everything to find what he needs most. Finally Drew could accept Ira's generous gift. Olivia.

The shutters rattled, reminding Olivia that a storm raged outside.

Feeling safe and secure, she decided to spill out the rest of her plot to seduce him, if necessary, to make him stay.

"I called Walt," she said, then watched Drew's eyes cloud with confusion until she added, "You remember—the mechanic from Stillwater?"

"How could I forget Walt?"

"Well, I asked Walt as a special favor if he could deliver a full-size bed. He couldn't come today, but he promised it would be here by tomorrow."

"In the meantime, we'll make do with a cot and a sleeping bag," he said with a crooked grin.

"Mmm." Before she could add anything, Drew silenced her with another ravaging kiss.

Perhaps for the first time in her entire life, Olivia forgot what she was going to say. With a soft smile, she wrapped her arms around him, surrendering all that she was and all that she could be to this man.

Finally he pulled away to gaze lovingly into her eyes.

"We've got plenty of food and wood for the fire," she murmured. "Maybe we'll get snowed in." She was obviously not too concerned.

He smiled rakishly. "We can only hope." He shook his head in admiration. He wondered what was coming next from her mixed bag of surprises. Life with Olivia promised to be unconventional and filled with excitement. "The first time I set eyes on you, I knew you were trouble."

"And I decided you were great husband material."

He laughed shortly. "You did not!"

Her eyes glowed with love. "Oh, yes, I did."

And he believed her.

*   *   *   *   *

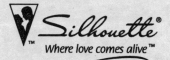

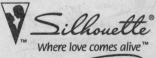

LINDSAY McKENNA

continues her popular series,

MORGAN'S MERCENARIES

with a brand-new, longer-length single title!

She had never needed anyone before. Never ached for a man before. Until her latest mission put Apache pilot Akiva Redtail in the hot seat next to army officer Joe Calhoun. And as they rode through the thunderous skies, dodging danger at every turn, Akiva discovered a strength in Joe's arms, a fiery passion she was powerless to battle against. For only with this rugged soldier by her side could this Native American beauty fulfill the destiny she was born to. Only with Joe did she dare open her heart to love....

"When it comes to action and romance, nobody does it better than Ms. McKenna."
—*Romantic Times Magazine*

Available in March from Silhouette Books!

Where love comes alive™

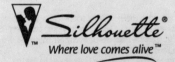